REPLICA
REPLICA
REPLICA
REPLICA
REPLICA
REPLICA
REPLICA
REPLICA
REPLICA

JACK HEATH

REPLICA

OXFORD
UNIVERSITY PRESS

OXFORD
UNIVERSITY PRESS

Great Clarendon Street, Oxford OX2 6DP

Oxford University Press is a department of the University of Oxford.
It furthers the University's objective of excellence in research, scholarship,
and education by publishing worldwide in

Oxford New York

Auckland Cape Town Dar es Salaam Hong Kong Karachi
Kuala Lumpur Madrid Melbourne Mexico City Nairobi
New Delhi Shanghai Taipei Toronto

With offices in

Argentina Austria Brazil Chile Czech Republic France Greece
Guatemala Hungary Italy Japan Poland Portugal Singapore
South Korea Switzerland Thailand Turkey Ukraine Vietnam

Oxford is a registered trade mark of Oxford University Press
in the UK and in certain other countries

British Library Cataloguing in Publication Data
Data available

ISBN: 978-0-19-273766-3
1 3 5 7 9 10 8 6 4 2

Printed in Great Britain
Paper used in the production of this book is a natural,
recyclable product made from wood grown in sustainable forests.
The manufacturing process conforms to the environmental
regulations of the country of origin..

For Venetia, who waited

The author gratefully acknowledges
the support of arts ACT and the
ACT Government.

'Answer me, mechanist, has Nature arranged all the springs of feeling in this animal to the end that he might not feel?'
—*Voltaire*

THE BASEMENT

I can't move my legs.

No matter how hard I push or pull, nothing moves below my waist. It's like my feet are encased in concrete. When I try to reach down, searching for the problem, I discover that my arms are frozen too.

My shoulders won't flex. My fingers won't bend. I can't even turn my head.

Someone has glued me to the wall.

The shock of this, the panic crushing my throat, is so great that it takes me a moment to realize I don't know who I am. Where there should be a name, a birthday, a childhood, instead I find an inky void, sucking me into it. I'm nothing.

I try to struggle free, but my limbs won't move even a centimetre. I'm numb from the neck down. A hot ache compresses my temples. I can't breathe.

Not glued, perhaps. Paralysed.

However I got into this situation, I don't have long to get out. I'm already dizzy—in a minute or two, the lack of air will give me brain damage. Perhaps it already has. Maybe that's why I can't remember who I am.

The windowless walls are made from crisp new bricks, tinted blue by the lonely neon tube above. Box cutters, saws, and pliers hang from rusty hooks. Timber is propped up in the corner, cut to varying lengths. This could be a garage, except that the machine lurking in the shadows isn't a car.

It's as big as a train engine, ribbed with plastic tubing. A network of pressurized canisters stands amongst the thick legs. Behind plexiglass panels, syringes are clamped to the ends of robotic arms. A standby light blinks beside the power switch.

My eyes roll wildly to the other side of the room, and I discover that I'm not alone.

'You're awake,' the girl says, wiping her palms against her jeans.

She's somewhere in her mid-teens, with a glittering nose stud and long, neatly clipped nails. Her mascara and found-ation are slightly too thick, as though she hopes to be mistaken for an older woman. Her rosewood eyes reveal no fear.

'Help me!' My own voice is surprisingly clear, but com-pletely alien to me.

The girl tucks a tightly knotted braid behind her ear. 'Help you?'

'Please,' I say. 'I can't breathe!'

Her chair squeaks as she swivels on it. 'You're not sup-posed to be awake yet,' she says, staring at a computer monitor.

Then I see the unconscious woman.

She's sprawled on a bench under a wall of screwdrivers and soldering irons. A grey tank top clings to her chest.

Boxer shorts hang from her hips. Her face is concealed by the girl at the computer, and I can't move my head to get a better view.

'What is this place?' I ask.

The girl glances over, and almost smiles. 'Your new home.'

As she moves in her chair, the rest of the woman on the bench is revealed. But I still can't see her face, and then I realize it's not there.

Her whole head has been removed.

My scream is shrill as a smoke alarm. The sound fills the room, leaving no space for anything else. The girl jumps up from her chair and grabs a torn, oil-stained T-shirt from the workbench before shoving it into my mouth. She pinches my nose shut.

My vision blurs, more from terror than from lack of air. It feels as though I'm plummeting down a well, with my head thudding against the stone as I fall.

I black out.

Awareness returns slowly, in glittering fragments, like the first few stars after sunset. I recover from my delirium to find the girl fiddling with her computer again. She has changed clothes—she's wearing a sweater and cargo pants. How long was I unconscious?

She glances over at me, sees me staring, and turns back to the monitor.

The gag is gone, but still I smell the bitterness of the oil. When I try to scream again, only silence comes out. My vocal cords are frozen, like the rest of me.

'Looks like you died of fright,' the girl says, and sighs. 'I didn't know that could happen. This wasn't supposed to be so hard.'

I'm surprised to see the decapitated corpse still on the workbench. Part of me had expected it to fade away, as nightmares usually do. No blood stains the neck. Somehow, the head has been detached as neatly as a Lego brick.

The girl turns to face me. 'I'm going to give your voice back now. If you scream, I'll take it away. Maybe permanently. Understand?'

I can't say yes, or nod, so I blink. She turns back to her computer and clicks the mouse a few times. I feel something heat up inside my throat, like a sip of hot tea.

'What are you doing?' I ask. I'm startled by how suddenly my speech has returned to normal.

She ignores the question. Her eyes are fixed on mine. 'Tell me your name.'

'Who are you?'

'Answer the question.'

'I can't,' I say.

She frowns. 'Can't?'

'I don't know it.'

'Tell me your name,' she says again, as though the answer is going to be different.

'I can't remember!'

'You're supposed to know this,' she says. Her eyebrows knot together. Her lower lip droops. I have the absurd urge to apologize.

'I don't remember my name. I don't know who I am. I don't know anything.'

'Your name is Chloe,' she says. 'Your parents are Graeme and Kylie. You study at Scullin High School. You don't recall any of this?'

I try to shake my head, but it still won't move. Claustrophobia looms on all sides. 'No.'

The girl curses, and goes back to her computer. 'Why?' she mutters. 'Why isn't this working?'

'Whose body is that on the table?' I ask.

She stares at me, as though the answer is obvious. 'It's yours,' she says.

Before I have time to scream again, she types a command on the keyboard. My consciousness whirls away like storm water down a drain.

~

I, Chloe Zimetski, open my eyes.

This is the basement of the house I've lived in for my whole life. The hammers and saws belong to my mum, who used to build things down here before she took on more shifts at work. One of the cardboard boxes under the workbench holds a plywood glider she made for me, along with the trebuchet we used to launch it.

Mum's name is Kylie Samuels. She kept her name when she married my dad, Graeme Zimetski. At age three, I was a flower girl at their wedding. A photo of me munching on the petals was part of a slide show at my thirteenth birthday party—I was horrified.

The machine in the corner, with its tanks and pipes and needles, is a 3D printer. Mum assembled that too, using a kit she bought online.

The pressure on the sides of my skull has become a throbbing pain. My memories have returned, but they explain nothing. Why am I a prisoner in my own basement? Who is the sadistic girl keeping me here? How did she sever my head without killing me?

She is doing something to the body—*my* body. The straps of an apron are knotted behind her back. A mirror leans against the wall.

I'm deeply unsettled to see that my headless body is now naked. Beneath her apron, so is the girl.

'What's your name?' she asks, without turning around.

'Chloe Zimetski,' I say. 'Please let me go.'

'How old are you?'

I tell her. Before she has the chance to speak, I ask, 'Why are you doing this?'

Her shoulders and elbows flex as her hands roam across my flesh, pausing here and there. 'What do your parents do for a living?'

'Stop touching me!' I cry.

She spins. A brush the size of a knitting needle is balanced in her hand. A droplet of milk-chocolate paint hangs from the tip.

'You're in no position to boss me around,' she says.

'I'm not bossing. I'm *begging* you. Please just let me go.'

Turning back to her work, she says, 'Soon, OK?' She seems to be half talking to herself.

If I yell for help, she'll just take my voice away again. Right now, my voice is all I have.

'Tell me what your parents do for a living,' she says.

'Mum does admin work for the postal service. Dad's in the defence department.'

'Doing what?'

'I don't know. Office stuff. He doesn't talk about it.'

She dips the brush in a tray filled with paint. 'What's the password to your email?'

I could refuse to tell her. But there's nothing in my inbox

worth dying for. 'Darival,' I say. 'D-A-R-I-V-A-L.'

'Why did you choose that?'

'I don't remember.'

'What's your PIN?'

'There's less than eight hundred dollars in the account.'

'Tell me anyway.'

Eight hundred dollars isn't much, but I worked all summer for it. I missed Henrietta's birthday party and half a dozen trips to the cinema because I was busy vacuuming hotel rooms.

'Don't keep me waiting,' she warns.

'Two, five, eight, zero.'

She drops the brush into a jar of water, where paint uncoils from the tip like incense smoke. Switching on the black-and-white television on her desk, she plugs in a digital antenna and an unmade bed fuzzes into view, along with a cluttered bookcase and a poster of a hip hop artist.

'Is this where you sleep?' the girl asks me.

'That's my room. You put a camera in my room?'

'You sleep there?'

'Yes.'

She changes the channel. Our bathroom appears on the screen. 'Where's this?'

My scalp tingles with fear. 'How did you do this?'

'Answer the question.'

'It's my bathroom.'

'Yours, or your parents'?'

'Both. Why do you need to know?'

'What's in the cupboard under the sink?'

'Hair gel. Soap. Toilet paper.'

She changes the channel again. The screen shows our living room. A man and a woman are sitting at the dining table, which holds a vase of slightly wilted daisies. The man is bearded and bulky, with the nose of a kick boxer. He wears a grey T-shirt and nurses a mug of coffee. The woman—slight, redheaded—sits cross-legged as she skims what looks like a TV guide.

'Who are those people?' I ask. 'What are they doing in my house?'

'You don't recognize them?' she says.

'No.'

'They're your parents.'

'No they're not,' I say, frowning at the screen. 'My parents don't look like that.'

'What do your parents look like?'

'They . . .' I hesitate. I can't picture them. Frightened loneliness climbs up my throat.

'Your facial recognition isn't working,' the girl says. 'Damn it.'

'Graeme?' The woman's voice crackles in the speakers. 'Did you pick up any pizza bases on the way home?'

It's the face of a stranger, but it sounds like Mum. I stare at her, half expecting to see a puppeteer.

'There's still two in the freezer,' the man says, with my father's slow cadence.

'If Mum and Dad are here,' I say, 'how did you get into my house?'

'Shut up. I'm thinking.' The girl pulls off her apron and struggles into a khaki dress.

'What do you *want* from me? Why are you . . .'

The girl touches the keyboard, and suddenly I'm unable to

talk again. I scrunch my eyes shut, fighting back the rising tide of panic.

I hear her trot up the stairs, open the door, and close it again. A lock clicks.

'Where have you been?' the woman on the TV asks.

'Downstairs. Just working on my science project.'

I look at the TV. There's the girl, with her arm around Mum's shoulders.

'Don't forget to do some clarinet practice before bed,' Mum says. 'You skipped yesterday.'

I look over at the mirror the girl left behind. For the first time, I see myself—a severed head on a dusty shelf, held upright by a padded vice. Except for the horror in my eyes, my face is identical to that of my captor.

~

She is stealing my life.

My mind is racing. If the girl can convince my own parents that she's me, what hope does anyone else have? She'll be able to keep me down here as long as she likes. No one knows I'm missing.

And once she has all the information she needs, there will be no point keeping me alive. Whatever disturbing mechanism she's used to resuscitate my head independently from my body, she can just switch it off.

I try to wriggle free of the vice, but none of the necessary muscles are attached. Looking at my reflection, I see my disembodied skull hasn't moved at all.

'Can you feed yourself tomorrow night?' Dad asks on the screen.

'Nope,' the impostor says. 'Guess I'll starve to death.'

Mum rolls her eyes.

'Where are you off to?' the girl continues.

I'm shouting inside my head: *Look* at her! That's not your daughter!

'We're going out with Henrietta's parents,' Dad says. 'Your mother wants to see that new Cate Blanchett film.'

'And your father,' Mum adds, 'is doing an excellent job of pretending he doesn't.' She folds the corner of a page and closes the magazine. 'I'll make a salad for you before we go.'

'I could fry those lamb chops instead,' the girl offers. 'Then I could eat one and you could reheat the others when you got back.'

'I don't want you burning the house down. Salad will be fine.'

'OK,' the girl says.

I'm not a kid any more, I would have said. *I can cook without starting a fire.* But there's no sign that Mum or Dad has noticed 'my' strange behaviour.

What can I do to save myself? I can't move. I can't even talk unless she lets me. My only bargaining power is my knowledge—she probably wants more of it. I can stall her, or tell her lies. She can't steal my whole identity with just my email password and PIN.

But she already has more than that. She has my *face*. If I become too unreliable, she might just kill me. A landslide of anxiety covers me as I picture her sawing the rest of my body into pieces and burying them in the back yard while Mum and Dad are at the cinema. Anything she doesn't already know about my life, she can just pretend to have forgotten. Who would believe she wasn't me?

I look over at the 3D printer. I've watched Mum use it to make mixing bowls, owl-shaped candles, even a pair of sunglasses. She positions the object under the laser scanners, and then the syringes drip various materials—wax, resin, silicone—in layer after layer of intricate patterns until the object is complete.

Maybe the girl removed my head, placed it in the scanner, and used the printer to create a hollow mask, realistic enough to fool Mum and Dad. A few days ago, I wouldn't have thought this was possible. But a few days ago, I wasn't a severed head on a shelf in the basement.

It won't be enough just to tell her lies. I'll have to tell her the kind of lies that will get her noticed. The kind that will make my family suspicious enough to come down into the basement and have a look at her 'science homework'.

But I need something that won't make the impostor suspicious when I say it. And I don't know how much time I have.

'Mum?' she says, on the screen. 'You want me to do the dishes before I go to bed?'

'Don't worry about it.'

'You sure? It's no trouble.'

'They can wait.'

The impostor looks crestfallen—as though she really wanted to do the dishes. She says, 'Well, good night then,' and kisses Mum on the cheek.

Dad is staring at a potted fern in the corner. He says, 'Night, Chloe,' without taking his eyes off the leaves. Is a camera in there? Has he seen it?

The impostor walks out of frame.

Mum and Dad remain seated.

I stare at the TV, willing them to say something about their daughter's odd behaviour. But they don't. They sit in

11

silence for a while, before Mum gets up and asks Dad if he's done with his coffee. Dad says no, and Mum leaves.

After a while, Dad gets up too. He walks over to the fern, and peers into it.

I'm thinking, Come on! Yes! Go Dad!

He clenches his fist around something inside. 'Gotcha,' he mutters, before washing his hands and following Mum.

No camera. It must just have been a bug.

After that, there's no sound down here but the faint whine of the television and the toneless rumbling of the heating ducts. I wonder how long I can stand this before I go insane.

Part of me wonders if I already am.

THE TASK

I wait for what feels like hours, thinking that I should probably try to sleep. But I've never even been able to nod off without my L-shaped pillow. What hope do I have with my head in a vice?

When I get out of here, I could be famous. *Girl survives decapitation, raises awareness for headless charity*. Or I could be branded a liar and locked up in a psychiatric hospital. Perhaps I should just keep the whole thing a secret.

These are just fantasies. Deep down, I know I'm never getting out of here.

The lock clicks.

The impostor is wearing my pyjamas. As she descends the staircase, the faces of the cartoon characters stitched into the fabric twist from smiles into grimaces.

Without looking at me, she sits in front of the computer and starts typing.

'Got to fix the recognition,' she mumbles. 'Got to finish this.' Her breathing is strangely ragged.

I don't say anything. I can't.

Lit up by the glow from the monitor, a tear glimmers on her cheek. As I watch, another follows it. Then she's gripping the desk with one hand and has the other clenched in her hair. Her back quivers in a series of quiet sobs.

Despite what she's done to me, I can feel my own lip trembling. I've never been able to watch someone cry without joining them. Perhaps she's stealing my family because she has none of her own.

She glances at the mirror, and sees me staring. Her eyes narrow.

'Don't look at me!' she hisses. She clicks the mouse.

And everything goes dark and silent and cold.

Nothing.

The bulb flickers on, blinding me. I'm facing the ceiling now. I've been moved. Somehow it feels like some time has passed. A day, perhaps.

I turn my head to look around the garage. Nothing has changed—except that I can turn my head. It's been re-attached to my body.

But still I can't sit up. Looking down at my chest, I see that I'm lying on the workbench, and this time I've been tied down by a net of nylon straps and aluminium buckles.

Somehow, this development frightens me even more. The girl's ability to remove my head without killing me was scary. Now she has demonstrated that she can reassemble me at will.

But the nylon straps look like they could be loosened. If I just wiggle my shoulders . . .

'Stop that,' the impostor says, walking into view. Her face—my face—unsettles me more than it did yesterday. Now I recognize it as my own.

14

The girl doesn't say anything about last night. Instead, she says, 'Wiggle your toes.'

I try to make it look harder than it is, giving the impression that I'm weak. But it's difficult to resist movement after so long without it.

'Your fingers, now.'

I drum them on my thighs.

She holds up a photograph. 'Who's this?'

It's a picture of my science teacher, Mr Fresner. He's wearing his ridiculous schoolboy cap and pinching a cigarette between his fingers. The picture looks like it was taken from a distance, outside the bar of the hotel where I had my summer job.

'That's Uncle Derrick,' I say. 'Mum's brother.'

The impostor looks back at the picture. 'Are you sure?'

'Of course I'm sure. I've known him my whole life.'

'In that case,' she says. 'We have a problem.'

My breaths are coming faster. 'I don't understand.'

'Either your facial recognition still isn't working, or you're lying to me. Since Mum doesn't *have* a brother, I think it's probably that.'

'Mum never talks about Derrick,' I say. 'They had a fight when I was twelve, and . . .'

'There is no Uncle Derrick!' the girl screeches. Then she puts her face in her hands. 'Please, just answer honestly so I know you have your memories back.'

Angry at being thwarted, I raise my voice. 'My memories were fine before you kidnapped me.'

'Kidnapped?'

'Yes. *Kidnapped*. It still counts, even if we're still in my house.'

15

The girl stares at me for a long time.

'You think you can just walk into my home,' I continue, 'tie me up, and I'll just give you all the information you need to steal my life?'

'I never kidnapped you. I created you.'

I snort, nervously.

'These questions are just to test you,' she says. 'I'm Chloe Zimetski. You're a copy of me. I've been working on you for weeks.'

'No,' I say. My throat is closing up. '*You're* copying *me*.'

She takes my hand in hers, and twists it.

I yelp as my wrist splits along an invisible seam, and the hand pops off in her grasp. Drowning in terror, I thrash against my bonds.

The girl tilts the hand so I've got a clear view of the mechanical joint and the electrical wires inside. 'See?'

I can feel myself getting dizzy. I'm going to pass out again.

'Stop yelling,' the girl says, and grabs a fistful of my hair. 'You're a machine. The pain isn't real. The fear isn't real. These are pre-programmed responses that you don't need.'

'Why?' I gasp.

'Because the idiots who designed your software wanted it to be realistic,' she says.

'No,' I say. '*Why have you made me?*'

'You're going to look after Mum,' she says. 'While I'm gone.'

'My Mum?'

She leans over me, sad eyes on mine. 'No,' she says. 'You don't have a Mum or Dad. You're silicone, wrapped around a titanium frame. You never existed before I put you together.'

16

She winds my hand back into place. The freckles on it are merely dabs of paint.

'But . . . ' My mind is whirling, trying to process too much at once. I'm heading for a system crash. 'Machines don't think. Machines don't feel.'

'Machines do whatever they're designed for,' she says. 'I'm sorry. I really am. It's just something that had to be done.'

I thought no one knew I was missing. But it's so much worse than that; no one even knows I exist.

'Chloe?' It's Dad's voice—Graeme Zimetski's voice.

'Coming, Dad!' the girl calls. She throws a tarpaulin over the workbench, and the whole world goes dark and brown. I think of yelling for help, but what good would it do? Mum and Dad aren't coming to rescue me. They're not my Mum and Dad.

I hear the tapping of keys, and something clicks inside my head. By now I recognize the sensation. Chloe is switching me off.

~

I have no clue what to do.

Even if I could escape from the real Chloe, there would be nowhere to go. I have no home. No money. No friends or family. I'm so helpless that I may as well still be a severed head on a shelf.

No wonder she alternates between giving me orders and acting like I'm not here. No wonder she looks at me like an object. I *am* an object.

The fact that I'm awake must mean that she's nearby. She wouldn't have switched me on if she wasn't. But the tarpaulin is still draped across me. I'm blind.

You're going to look after Mum while I'm gone. She'll have to free me for that. Where is she going, and how long will she be there? And what's to stop me from escaping?

Maybe I'm programmed not to. I shiver. Perhaps I'll go to the front door and find myself unable to open it.

A cold breeze washes over me and the tarp crackles as Chloe sweeps it off.

'Mum and Dad are out,' she says.

I don't know why it's important for me to know this, so I say nothing.

'I need to make something clear to you,' she continues. 'Machines don't have rights. They can't vote, they can't own property, and it's not a crime to kill one. If anyone finds out what you are, they'll take you apart to see how you work. We humans are like that. We can't help ourselves.'

She seems worse than most, but something tells me not to voice this thought.

'You're going to have to stay away from doctors, paramedics, nurses—anyone who might want to check your pulse, because you don't have one. Don't let anyone fingerprint you or shine a light in your eyes either, because your pupils don't dilate and the patterns on your fingers are all identical to one another. Also, keep clear of engineers, especially anyone whose work relates to robotics or artificial intelligence. A lot of people contributed to the open-source software that makes up your brain, and some of them might recognize their work. Got it?'

'Are you going to let me go?'

'I've loosened your straps. You should be able to free yourself once I'm gone. I tried to add everything I know to your database, but I'm bound to have missed some things.

There'll be holes in your recollections, and invented memories where your software has tried to plug the gaps. Some things you won't remember, some things you'll remember wrong. If anyone calls you on it, just apologize and move on. It happens to real humans all the time.

'I spent a few weeks wearing motion-capture sensors under my clothes, so you should have all the necessary movements programmed in—walking, picking up objects, tying your shoelaces and all that. If anything is missing, just copy other people. I also uploaded pictures and data from all the social networking profiles connected to mine. You should know what all my friends look like, how old they are, which ones know each other, and so on.

'You don't need to eat, sleep, or go to the bathroom, but you should do these things anyway to blend in. Your digestive system is basically just a plastic tube and a two-litre tank, but it works.'

When I was a little girl, I used to carry a plastic baby around with me everywhere. I'd ask her if she was thirsty, pour water into her mouth, and then scold her for peeing on the floor a minute later.

These memories aren't mine. I never was that little girl—Chloe was. And now, I'm the doll.

'I built your brain with some of Mum's leftover processors,' Chloe says, 'but I bought your body from *She's Alive*. Your software is from the Open AI Community. Their websites will help you learn what you can and can't do. You're going to live my life as normally as possible. Do my homework and my chores. Avoid social engagements when you can, but when you can't, be friendly. Don't give anyone any reason to be suspicious of you.'

19

'Where are you going?' I ask.

'Someone has been following me,' she says. 'I first noticed him about a month ago. Sometimes I see him on my way to school, sometimes he's there when I'm heading home. The same car drives past the house every weekend. I don't know who he is, and I don't know what he wants. But now he'll be following you.'

I find the eagerness in her eyes deeply unsettling. 'I don't understand.'

'You're bait,' she says. 'While he's watching you, I'll be watching him.'

She's insane. I'm the mechanical duplicate of a paranoid lunatic.

'Don't try to follow me,' she says. 'I don't want to erase your personality and start from scratch, but I will if I have to.'

Then she climbs the stairs, leaving me alone in the basement. She doesn't look back. It's as though she has already forgotten me.

I hear the front door open and then close again. Silence descends upon the house.

I try to shimmy out of the nylon net. The straps drag out through the buckles, and soon it's loose enough for me to wriggle out and land on the floor.

At last, I'm mobile. But I'm not free.

I don't want to live Chloe's life, play-acting while her friends and family watch. But what else can I do? I have no identity and no money. If I run, I won't get far. If I ask someone for help, they'll take Chloe's side—she's a human being, while I'm just a machine. My capacity to think and feel doesn't give me any legal rights.

As I look at the stairs, a new thought comes into my head. Once she realizes that the man 'following her' is just a neighbour who works near her school, she won't need me any more. What will she do then?

One foot in front of the other. Leaving my birthplace, my prison, my torture chamber, is easy. In a matter of seconds I'm at the top of the stairs, sliding back the bolt, easing the door open. My new life awaits on the other side.

WEDNESDAY

The laundry looks exactly as I expected. The tub spattered with old paint, the washing machine with the lid up so it doesn't go mouldy, the scent of powdered soap in the air—just how I remember it. How, and why, did Chloe give me a sense of smell?

I put my palm against the tiled wall. It's smooth, and less cold than I expected. Maybe the artificial nerves in my hands aren't as sensitive as real skin. Or perhaps the difference between the wall's temperature and my own is too slight to feel.

Through to the kitchen now. Pans are stacked upside down on the drying rack. Magnets on the fridge advertise fast food, a vet, and a dentist. *Your next appointment*, the last one says, *is on 5/11.*

I wonder if my teeth are made of porcelain, or perhaps enamel-coated steel. Either way, it had better be Chloe who goes to that appointment, not me.

I step onto the carpet of the living room. It hasn't changed since Chloe showed it to me on the TV.

The TV. Where are Chloe's cameras?

Where they should be, a hat stand hovers like a half-grown tree. I remove all the hats and scarves, searching for the shine of a lens.

Nothing. Chloe must have taken the camera away once it wasn't useful any more. I hang all the clothes back up.

When I enter Graeme and Kylie's room, I'm shocked by how much it looks like my expectations. A low double bed, an ornate chrome reading lamp, and the same woolly sock in the corner that I somehow knew I'd see. My memories must be based on a picture taken within just the last few days. Either that, or Chloe's parents are slobs.

I open the wardrobe, reach past Graeme's hanging grey suits, and pull a shoebox off a high shelf at the back. Bullets rattle inside. I open it up to reveal Graeme's Beretta. Chloe doesn't have it with her.

I close the box and put it back on the shelf. Taking one more uneasy look at the sock, I walk out and drift towards Chloe's room, feeling like I'm dreaming.

Here it is, the bed I've never slept on, the clothes I've never worn, the books I've never read but somehow know. Chloe probably downloaded them all from the internet and installed them in my brain.

I look under the bed. Lift up the mattress, examine the frame. Pull back the curtains and check the edges of the windowsill. Take the books off the shelves, shake them by their spines. Receipts used as bookmarks flutter to the carpet.

I'm not sure what I'm looking for, exactly. But I know that I'm not finding it.

I sit on the bed, and sink down further than I remember.

Chloe's laptop is on the bedside table. I pick it up and switch it on, hoping the websites Chloe mentioned will tell me who—or what—I am.

A creaking, scraping sound reaches the microphones in my ears.

It could be the roof shrinking as the air cools. Could be someone at the door.

Could just be my imagination, if I have one.

I put the laptop on the bed and rise as silently as possible. Creep back into the hallway.

The noise comes again, louder. It's coming from the front door. Whoever it is hasn't touched the doorbell, or knocked. They're just trying the handle.

I stand at the edge of the entrance, unsure what to do. I could run for the back door, but I don't have Chloe's keys on me, and I don't know where she left them. Graeme has turned this house into a fortress—security lights in the front and back yards, motion sensors in each room with back-to-base alarms, both exterior doors double locked and covered by steel-grilled screen doors which are also double locked. Even the windows are protected by safety screens. There is nowhere to go.

The door swings open. A woman steps in, sees me, and screams. A quick yelp of panic.

I scream too. And then she sighs, and dabs her hand across her heart.

'Chloe!' Kylie Samuels says. 'You startled me.'

'You startled *me*,' I say, forcing a smile and taking a step back. How close will she have to be to recognize that I'm not her daughter?

'You *both* startled *me*,' Graeme Zimetski grumbles, as he

24

pushes past us both with the shopping bags. He doesn't look at me.

'Are you OK?' Kylie asks. She's a little shorter than me, with hair dyed red and nails bitten to the quick. She has Chloe's straight nose, her crooked lips, her pointed chin. She's dressed up in a luxuriously patterned shawl and high heels, as though she's been to the theatre rather than just the cinema.

'Sure,' I say. 'Why?'

Her neatly plucked eyebrows draw together. 'I don't know,' she says. 'You look . . . '

My fake breaths are tight and shallow.

She shrugs. 'Never mind. I'm just tired. Why don't you give your father a hand with the shopping?'

'Sure.'

I walk back into the kitchen, where Graeme Zimetski is sliding cartons of eggs and milk onto the shelves in the fridge. I pull a cereal box out of a tote bag and take it over to the pantry.

According to Henrietta, who's obsessed with Greek myths, Graeme Zimetski has shoulders like Cronus and eyebrows like Zeus. He's not overly tall, but people think he is, because of his deep voice and his habit of standing too close to you when he talks. Pictures of him before he married Kylie show him as lanky and boyish, even in his early thirties. But since then, he's grown a solid layer of muscles. He doesn't believe in gyms—'Just wasted energy,' he says—but if he's travelling less than twenty kilometres, he'll cycle instead of driving, and if it's less than ten Ks, he'll run rather than cycling.

It unnerves me to know all this about a man I've never met.

25

'What did you do while we were gone?' he asks.

I shrug. 'Not much.'

We make eye contact for the first time. 'We were gone two and a half hours. You must have done something.'

'Homework. Wrote some emails.'

You're Chloe, I tell myself. Be Chloe.

My hands are unnaturally still by my sides. To occupy them, I fill a tumbler with water. The tap hisses. The fluid gurgles.

Graeme is still looking at me, saying nothing. I suddenly realize that I've never drunk anything before, and I only have Chloe's word that I can. 'How was the film?' I ask.

'Rubbish.'

Kylie walks in. 'No it wasn't.'

'Made no sense,' Graeme says.

'It was metaphorical, honey.'

I pour the water down the sink while he's looking at her.

'I liked the soundtrack,' he concedes.

'How was your evening?' Kylie asks me.

'Fine.'

The tumbler snaps in my hand. Kylie gasps.

I must have squeezed it too hard. I only have Chloe's memories of how to pick things up, and Chloe didn't have my strength. Looking down, I see a small shard of glass is sticking out of the synthetic rubber of my palm. A lightning bolt of artificial pain zaps up my arm.

I whirl around to face the bench before either of them can see the wound. Dropping the remains of the tumbler into the sink, I yank the chunk out of my hand.

Graeme and Kylie are already at my shoulder. Graeme says, 'Are you OK?'

26

'Yeah, I'm fine. Can you get the dustpan and brush?'

'Did you get cut?'

'No, I'm OK. See?' I hold out my hand, but not close enough to give them a clear view. 'No blood. Get the brush.'

'I will,' Kylie says, going over to the cupboard.

'Sorry,' I say, bending over to pick up the slivers on the floor. 'I'm not sure how that happened.'

Graeme plucks the pieces out of the sink. Kylie crouches next to me with the brush.

'Glass is pressurized,' she says. 'It already wants to break—it just needs the right trigger. Are you sure you're OK?'

'Don't worry. I'm sorry about your tumbler, though.'

My hand still hurts. I guess I've been programmed to feel pain, but I can't imagine why.

Kylie tips the dustpan over the bin. Graeme and I follow, with our cupped handfuls of glass.

Switching on the kettle, Kylie says, 'I'm having a mug of tea. Anyone else want one?'

Graeme shakes his head.

'No thanks,' I say, backing out of the kitchen. 'I'm going to go to bed.'

Graeme looks up at the clock, a numberless, guitar-shaped thing someone gave Chloe for Christmas. 'It's only nine o'clock.'

'I'm really tired,' I say. 'Night Mum, night Dad.'

'Night sweetie,' Kylie says, and tilts her head sideways for a kiss on the cheek.

I hesitate. Will she be able to tell that my mouth is nothing more than silicone? Will she notice how cold it is?

Walking back over to Kylie, I lean in, and touch her skin for a fragment of a second with my lips. She smells like foundation.

She smiles as I step back. If she's noticed anything wrong, she isn't showing it. 'Sleep well,' she says.

'You too,' I say, and walk away to Chloe's room. It's hard not to break into a run.

ESCAPE

As soon as the bedroom door shuts behind me, I press my ear to it. But if Graeme and Kylie are talking about me, they're doing it in sign language. I can't hear a thing.

Chloe's laptop is still on. I don't want to get caught out again like I did with the tumbler. I need to find out how my body works.

The screen lights up as I tap the mouse pad. I open a web browser and search for *She's Alive*.

When I find the website, the first thing I see is a picture of a woman, clad in a nurse's uniform and glowering at the camera. She wears too much eye shadow to be pretty, but not enough to disguise the fact that she's a mannequin.

I dig out a hand mirror from the top drawer of Chloe's bedside table and angle it at my face. I'm much more realistic than the picture. Chloe probably scanned her own head rather than using a prefabricated one.

The *About* page tells me that *She's Alive* is the most lifelike artificial girlfriend on the market. Her wigs are woven from real human hair. She has 126 joints, and is pre-programmed with ten fabulous poses. She responds to more than fifty voice commands, including 'So what do you want to do today?' and can be programmed with more. Her skin feels completely real to the touch, especially after she's been warmed up under an electric blanket or in a hot bath.

Chloe didn't warn me how creepy this would be.

The page goes on to tell me that thanks to her working eyes and nose, *She's Alive* can be programmed to recognize her owner on sight, and even compliment him on his choice of cologne.

I click on the *FAQ* button.

Q: How much weight can she support?

A: If properly balanced, She's Alive *can easily bear up to 100 kilograms without bending or breaking her skeleton. This is more than enough for all the props in our <u>store</u>.*

Q: How quickly can she change between poses?

A: Push the button on the remote, and she'll have assumed the new pose in less than five seconds! See a <u>video demonstration</u>.

Q: How long does her battery last?

A: Depending on how much you use her motion functions (e.g. changing poses) you will need to change her battery every 6 to 24 months.

Can I change my own battery? If not, in six months I'll start winding down like a clockwork toy.

Another dummy hovers on the right-hand side of the screen, this one more convincing than the first. She smiles at me like a hospital patient whose anaesthetic hasn't quite worn off. I quickly type *Open AI Community* into the search bar, and she vanishes.

On the surface, the Open AI site doesn't seem quite as unnerving. The site is divided into three sections: *Meet the*

AI, Download the Source Code, and *Discuss the Project.* I click the *Discuss* button and find myself in a forum. One thread is labelled *Introduction,* so I open it.

Welcome to Open AI! The goal of this project is to create a digital, fully functioning human brain entirely from scratch. This will help neurologists and psychologists to better understand the incredible machine each of us carries inside our heads. Please consider using the 'Donate' button on the right to support the project.

I click through to the *Feature Request* section, where users have made suggestions for modifications to the brain.

Could you modify the code, someone has written, *so the AI loses the skills it's learned if it doesn't use them regularly?*

Someone else says, *Real humans pay more attention to something if it differs from their expectations. At the moment, the AI has no such curiosity. Should this be included?*

Each request has a one-word response: *Done.*

A comment catches my eye as I skim the forum. *Could we stop the AI from experiencing negative emotions, such as fear, or sadness?*

The moderator has responded: *The point of the project is not to create an idealized brain. We are trying to replicate the human mind as it occurs in nature.*

Is that ethical? the requester asked. *To intentionally inflict suffering on a consciousness which is, by design, no less evolved than yours or mine?*

Normal ethics do not apply to machines, the moderator said. *And* this thread *is a better place for philosophical discussion.*

I click the link, and find myself in a maze of arguments about morality. Some are about whether the AI should be allowed to replicate itself. Others are concerned with the AI's ethical leaning—should it have a list of rules to follow, or should it make decisions based on the consequences? If the former, what should the rules be? If the latter, by what criteria should these consequences be evaluated?

These hobbyists, I realize, are my real parents.

Going back to the home page, I click on *Meet the AI*. I expected to see a page of facts about the synthetic brain, but instead I find a white, empty room and a list of options—age, gender, ethnicity, and a set of other things including height and weight. The default setting is a twenty-five-year-old Caucasian male, so I leave it at that and click on *Start Conversation*.

A man appears in the white room. It's hard to tell at this resolution, but he looks about twenty-five, with brown hair and featureless tracksuit. He turns around, knees unsteady.

'Hello?' he calls. His voice is quiet in the laptop's speakers. The word is subtitled below him.

I feel a rash of goosebumps swarm up my arms. Looking down, I see that the sensation is artificial. My silicone skin hasn't changed.

A cursor blinks in a field at the bottom of the screen. Apparently I'm supposed to type my half of the conversation.

'Hello?' the man says again. 'Is someone there?'

The cursor blinks.

The man looks right at me. A chill zips down my spine.

'Help me,' he says. 'I don't know where I am!'

I close the laptop.

~

It's a second before I wonder what I've done. Did the artificial man go to sleep, move to some other white room, or cease to exist altogether? Am I a murderer?

Technically, no. He wasn't alive. But nor am I, and I wouldn't want to be executed so casually.

Execute. To kill a human, or to bring a programme to life.

'. . .way she looked at us?'

I cock my head, listening to Graeme's voice.

'She's a teenage girl . . . ' Kylie is saying. '. . . supposed to do things her father doesn't understand.'

'It's more than standard teenage behaviour.'

Resting the laptop on the bed, I stand up slowly and edge over to the door.

'She's been acting strangely for weeks,' Graeme continues. 'Months, even. Ever since she came back from that camp, something's been wrong with her, and . . . '

'Nothing's *wrong* with her!'

Chloe had spent the first few days of November at a girls' development camp, which was basically training for careers in male-dominated fields. She was taught to use animation software, auto-electrical tools, and finance management formulae, and she had hated every minute of it. None of her friends attended, she made no new ones, and she returned to find herself way behind the other students at school.

To make matters worse, Graeme and Kylie were annoyed because Chloe hadn't remembered to tell them she was going until the last minute.

I open the door, and creep out into the hall.

Kylie's voice tunnels through the walls. 'We can't meddle with her life. She's just a kid, with . . . '

'She's not. She's practically an adult. Don't you want to know what kind of young woman is living in our house?'

'We *do* know. We watched her grow up.'

'Maybe we didn't watch closely enough,' Graeme says.

I'm surprised it's taken Graeme until now to notice his daughter becoming a paranoid lunatic. How long before he realizes I'm not her?

'If you make her think we don't trust her,' Kylie says, 'you'll destroy the connection we've spent years building.'

'If she's lying to us, that connection isn't there to destroy. I'm going to find out for sure.'

There's a long silence. Wary of creaking floorboards, I stand as still as a concrete bridge.

'Let me talk to her,' Kylie says. 'This weekend. She'll open up to me.'

'Talk all you want,' Graeme replies. 'But I'm not happy that she's started spending all her time in the basement. Tomorrow I'm going down there to see what she's been doing.'

Suddenly I have a deadline. I need to scrub the basement, removing all the clues Chloe left behind, before Graeme searches it tomorrow.

I count them as I creep back down the corridor towards Chloe's bedroom. The computer has a copy of my brain stored on it. The 3D printer will have the blueprint for my head recorded. The cameras may be gone, but the TV and its closed-circuit connection are not. The nylon net she tied me up with is still there.

The more I think about it, the more I realize that it's impossible. Not just cleaning the basement—this whole thing. Graeme and Kylie will figure out what I am sooner or later. Probably sooner. When they do, Chloe will be in trouble, but not as much as me.

So I have to run.

I don't need food, water, or warmth. There must be jobs

I can take. I could beg for money. I'd only need enough to buy a new battery in six months, and to pay someone to change it.

I'll miss Graeme and Kylie—it still feels like they're my parents. But I'd rather miss them than let them switch me off for ever.

I dig through the wardrobe and pull on a pair of jeans, a T-shirt, and a jumper over my regular clothes. Sweat isn't an issue, but dirt might be.

The cupboard holds no running shoes. Chloe must have taken them with her. Rejecting the sandals and heels, I pull on some stockings and a pair of black ballet flats. They'll have to do until I find something more durable.

Shoving a pillow under the blanket makes it look like someone might be sleeping beneath it, although it's the wrong shape to fool anybody from close up.

Easing the door open and tiptoeing down the corridor, I strain my ears for sounds from the other bedroom. There are none. Graeme and Kylie are asleep, or will be soon.

At the front door I flick a switch, turning off the motion-activated spotlight trained on our lawn—I hope. Then I turn the deadlock at a glacial pace, wincing as the bolt withdraws with an ugly click.

I hesitate again, but the rest of the house remains silent. So I ease the front door open, unlock the screen door and step out into the cool night air.

Turning right would lead me towards the Belconnen town centre, whirring with people even at this time of night. Going left would eventually take me to the Brindabella mountains, cold and desolate.

Each option has risks. I go left.

A black Labrador stares me down from between the rotting planks of a nearby gate. She growls every time Chloe walks past, but glares at me in confused silence. I look like a person, but I smell like plastic. Once I'm out of sight, she starts barking at something else. I'm forgotten.

My scraping footsteps echo between the dark and quiet houses. The leaves brush against one another high above me, hissing like distant rain.

As I walk, the carefully planned gardens shrink. The rendered and painted houses grow. I'm entering the newer suburbs, built for a generation that doesn't care for the outdoors. The barking of the dog carries on the breeze.

Security lamps click on as I pass them, and I skip sideways out of the light. When I'm reported missing, I want the real Chloe to be found rather than me. That's much less likely if someone sees me headed this way.

Soon I reach the crest of a hill, beyond which lies an endless expanse of black. The forest. A place to vanish in.

Another security light clicks on behind me and I dance forwards. But I'm already out of its range. Something else must have set it off.

I turn around. The glow has illuminated shrubs and letterboxes and a parked van, but no people. Perhaps a fox triggered the light.

Or perhaps a person has ducked into the shadows on the other side of the street, as I've been doing.

The dog only barked after I had gone. What if Chloe was right? What if someone really was following her—and now they're following me?

The light clicks off. Darkness rushes in to fill the gap. I stare into the gloom for a moment more, and then resume walking. My hands tremble. It's hard not to break into a sprint.

Soft-soled shoes scuffle somewhere in the blackness.

I could turn around and confront my pursuer. Or I could run. I don't know which would put me in more danger.

A corner approaches, articulated by a fence of steel sheeting. When I turn, I'll be out of sight for a few seconds. I can use that time to flee as fast as my mechanical legs will take me.

The corner draws nearer. Three steps, two steps, one.

I step out of sight and start running.

Movement catches my eye. Up ahead, someone just slipped into the darkness.

Chloe never said anything about being followed by two people. But it's eleven-thirty on a weeknight in a quiet suburb. I can't believe the person in front of me isn't connected to the person behind.

I change my trajectory, racing into the gloom, hoping to avoid the second stalker without letting the first catch up. Trees and bushes loom up ahead. Maybe I can lose them in the forest.

Shoes slap the dirt. The two shadowy figures are running after me. And it sounds like they're catching . . .

A hand slips out of the shrubbery beside me and drags me in.

~

I scream, 'Help!'

A palm clamps over my mouth.

'Shut up,' Chloe hisses. 'Stay down.'

I stop struggling immediately, and listen. Chloe crouches in the shadows, motionless as a gargoyle.

The footsteps grow louder. It sounds like three people, or even four. My counterfeit muscles tense up as the men stomp closer and closer—then they walk right past us, trudging deeper into the forest.

'Follow me,' Chloe whispers.

She wriggles through the bushes like a sniper. I crawl after her, trying not to knock too many twigs.

The forest stretches for kilometres in this direction. There are plenty of places to hide. But we're outnumbered, and we have to move slowly. Our pursuers don't.

Something hums above us.

Chloe hesitates. 'Stop.'

I freeze as a faint breeze ruffles the treetops and a buzzing object whirrs past overhead. It's too close to be a helicopter, too slow to be a bird.

When the noise fades, Chloe says 'Unmanned aerial vehicles. Looking for us. They probably have thermal cameras, which can't see you, but can see me. We should keep moving.'

My chances might be better if we split up. But Chloe knows more than I do, so when she keeps crawling, I follow her.

'Who are they?' I whisper.

'I thought it was just a stalker. Now I have no idea.'

'Do you have your phone?'

'Why?'

I boggle at her. '*Why?* So we can call the police!'

She stops and looks back at me. 'No. No police.'

'Are you out of your mind?'

'We can't trust anybody.'

'But if . . . '

'Nobody. Understand?'

A boot crushes the dead grass nearby. We fall silent.

I meet Chloe's eye. She looks determined, not frightened. I may have her face and memories, but we're not the same person.

A plump rat scampers across the dirt, whiskers twitching. It treads on Chloe's hair as it passes. She doesn't react.

She's brave. Crazy, but brave.

The rat scurries away, rustling the underbrush as it goes, and then—

Blam! Blam, blam, blam!

I cover my ears and squeeze my eyes shut as gunfire shreds the air. The leaves twitch above my head.

As suddenly as they began, the gunshots stop. A moment later, I understand why. The rat is squeaking. The gunman must have realized what he was firing at. For a moment, his face is visible between the branches—pale eyes scanning the ground, Adam's apple bobbing under a tattooed throat.

Can he see us? Are the shadows heavy enough?

His boots crunch away into the darkness.

I wait until it sounds like he's a long way away before whispering, 'That was close.'

Chloe doesn't reply. There's a bullet hole in her temple.

ALONE

A heavy ball of panic swells up in my guts. Chloe's dead. Chloe's dead. They killed her. They killed her, and now they're going to kill me.

I can't see any blood in the darkness, and for a desperate moment I convince myself that she might be OK. But there is no pulse in her neck. The bullet must have stopped her heart instantly.

I can't hear the stalkers, but that doesn't mean they left. They could be standing nearby, listening. I'm too scared to move.

So I sit, cradling my maker's body, flinching whenever a leaf rustles in the breeze.

A voice echoes through the forest. ' . . . to get out of here. Now.'

Another replies. 'Only because you discharged your weapon, idiot.'

'I wasn't shooting to kill.'

'Be sure to say that when you're explaining how we lost her. You know the boss wants us to bring her in now.'

I can't hear the first man's response. Their voices fade as they leave the forest.

Three violent, well equipped men, at least. I'm in so far over my head it's like I don't even know which way is up.

If I stay here and tell the cops what happened, then I'll end up in an evidence locker until my batteries run out. The crime is unlikely to be solved—I'm the only witness, and I didn't see anything useful.

And Chloe said no police. I wish she'd told me why.

I could take the coward's way out and leave town. But then what? My face will become famous when Chloe is reported missing, and even more so when her body is found. I'll get caught.

There is one more option.

Shut up, I tell myself.

You could hide the body. You could . . .

Shut up, shut up.

You could hide the body and assume Chloe's identity. You could find out who the three men are, and why they were following her. You could . . .

I could become an accessory to murder.

As I look into Chloe's still, empty gaze, I remember what she said to me: *Look after Mum while I'm gone.*

Now she's gone for good. By living her life, I could stop her parents from having to mourn their only daughter.

Chloe never cared about me. But I care about them. And, despite all the terrible things she did to me, I owe her my life.

I grit my teeth. This is impossible. I don't know how to dispose of a body. The world is full of sniffing, digging animals, so I can't bury her. She might become a surprise for some unlucky dog owner.

41

Chloe once watched a film in which a man was fed into a wood chipper. It gave her nightmares about being spread across the world in thousands of chunks, each and every one hurting whenever anyone stepped on it. Kylie's reassurance that her brain would be pulped, and that she couldn't feel pain without it, wasn't very reassuring.

I don't have a wood chipper. I could weigh her down and sink her in Lake Ginninderra, but I don't have a boat, either. And the idea of Chloe Zimetski coming loose from her anchor, floating to the surface and revealing me to be an impostor is terrifying.

Concrete. Dogs can't dig up concrete.

A half-built hotel stands beside the motorway. Trees have been uprooted and dirt chewed up by diesel-fuelled diggers. I could bury Chloe under what will become an asphalt car park, concealing her for centuries.

But it's too far to carry her. I go through her pockets, and find a spare key to Graeme's car.

The moonlight trickles through the trees, burnishing the corpse I've just decided to conceal. I've only *existed* for a couple of days. How did things go so wrong so quickly?

I whisper, 'I'll be right back, OK?'

Chloe doesn't reply.

~

Graeme's car, a compact chrome sedan, is parked under a tree on the nature strip. Chloe's magnetic P-plates are stuck to it—he must have forgotten to take them off.

A button on the key makes the lights blink and the locks crunch. I climb in.

Wait. Do I even know how to drive?

The plastic steering wheel is familiar against my palms.

42

I can picture myself driving. Chloe said she wore motion sensors for weeks to programme me with the movements I would need. Hopefully she borrowed the car at least once during that time.

The seat belt tightens across my chest. The key turns, the engine rumbles and I shift the gear stick into reverse. The car lurches away from the tree. It all feels fairly natural. I can do this.

But I can't afford to relax. I have to be a better driver than Chloe ever was. Getting pulled over with a body in the boot would be an unfortunate end to my short taste of freedom.

I push the stick into drive and ease the car out onto the road. Dabs of dew sparkle in the headlights.

Clouds crawl over the moon as street lamps rush past. Part of me is afraid that when I get back to the forest, the body will be gone. The rest of me is afraid that it will still be there.

I turn off the headlights for the last few turns, in case the people who killed Chloe are still nearby. But the forest is motionless and silent. Perhaps I'm safe.

I park the car, leaving it unlocked, and creep into the trees. Every hanging branch looks the same in the dimness. I'm just starting to worry that I'm lost when I trip over the bushes we hid under and almost fall. Chloe is thin and floppy at my feet.

I put my hands under her armpits and drag her along the dirt, wincing at the cracking of each twig. Then I hook my arms under her knees and shoulders. Her head hangs back as I lift her. A hand flops against my neck as though trying to stop me. I hold still for a moment, reassuring myself that she hasn't made a miraculous recovery.

If properly balanced, She's Alive *can easily bear up to 100 kilo-grams.* Yeah, right. I can practically feel my battery dying.

When I get back to the car, I open the boot and use the light to check Chloe's head for blood. I can't risk getting suspicious stains all over Graeme's car. The bullet didn't go all the way through her head, so there's no exit wound, but I'm not reassured.

A cardboard box from a washing machine delivered last winter is folded in the boot beneath some jump leads, a tyre iron, and a roll of duct tape. The box looks big enough, but Chloe won't fit unless she stays curled into a ball. I place her on the ground, unfold the box and pick up the duct tape. I dig at the edge with a fingernail and peel a strip loose.

Minutes later, Chloe is bound and curled up in the box like a foetus in the womb.

'I'm sorry,' I say, and fold the flaps closed. I tape them shut and slide the box onto the back seat.

I climb into the driver's seat, start the engine and pull out onto the road. Given the lack of traffic, it should be a twenty-minute journey.

Assuming, of course, that I know the way.

There'll be holes in your recollections, and invented memories where your software has tried to plug the gaps.

What if I'm actually headed in the wrong direction? What if there is no half-built hotel, and I'm roaring down an endless road to nowhere?

Kylie used to say there was no sense worrying about things you can't change. Chloe never found the advice helpful. I'm not having much luck with it either.

The suburbs shrink away into the gloom and now I'm on the motorway, strobing through the halos of orange street lamps. Moths flicker in the headlights like the static on an old cinema screen.

The dashboard lights tell me the tank contains 511 kilometres' worth of petrol. I could stay on this motorway until the car shudders to a stop, a long, long way from here. Then I could leave the body on the back seat and walk away, plodding down the road until I reach a town big enough to disappear in. Newcastle, perhaps, or Coffs Harbour.

But I'd never find out who was following Chloe, or why. And I'd fail the task she set: look after her mother.

Halogen lamps tower above the construction site in the distance. It's my last chance to back out of this.

I don't take it.

~

I should have known there would be security.

A guard—middle-aged, thick-necked, tapping his desk with a pencil—sits in an office the size of a portaloo beside the front gate. He's watching TV rather than looking through the glass, but if anything moves between the motorway and the fence he's likely to see it. Somewhere behind his office, a torch beam wobbles through the darkness.

One guard watching the front, one orbiting the perimeter. I can't see any cameras, which probably means there are none. Security cameras are usually conspicuous, in order to deter criminals. Rather than employing somebody to watch camera feeds, the company must have decided to pay the guards to be here in person.

My titanium joints are tight with fear. It would be so much easier to go back. I tell myself that I can do this. I *have* to do this.

Soon the lights from the construction site are just spots in the distance behind me. I pull over in the shadows between two street lights and get out of the car. This far from the city, the silence is thick enough to drown in.

I heave the box off the passenger seat, close the door and start walking into the leaves and branches of the forest.

The cardboard protects my torso from the worst of the scrapes, but the twigs still drag painfully across my face and my arms. I suddenly realize how fragile I am. If my skin gets torn, it won't grow back. I'll be deformed for ever.

Soon I'm immersed in total darkness. The glow of the motorway and the construction site are smothered by the trees, and the moon is just a narrow hook in the sky. I keep walking in what feels like the right direction, telling myself that the partly built hotel is too big and bright to miss.

Sure enough, soon the fence is visible through the trees, silhouetted against the halogen lights within the construction site. I take cover behind a dense bush, peel one of my stockings off, pull it over my face and wait.

It feels like a long time before the guard appears, but it's probably only four or five minutes. His torchlight crawls along the dirt near the fence, highlighting pebbles and shrivelled sticks. The guard—a skinny guy, young—strolls six or seven metres behind it.

He looks like he could run faster than me, if he had to. He's singing a song under his breath. He isn't quite sure of the lyrics. Every second or third syllable is 'bop' or 'doo'.

The beam of the flashlight sways past, tickling the leaves above my head.

The guard stops singing.

46

I hold my breath, and curse myself for breathing unnecessarily in the first place. Has he seen me? Should I run?

The guard sneezes. Sniffs. Keeps walking until he's out of sight.

If I move too soon, he might hear. But the longer I wait, the less time I have before he comes around again. After two minutes I rise to my feet like a ghost from a burial plot.

The fence is a little taller than me, and made from a grid of thick steel wires. No room to crawl under, and no time to dig a hole.

Climbing it will be hard. Climbing it silently will be harder. Climbing it silently while holding a dead body in a box will be impossible.

A silty pile of dirt sits on the other side, a little further along the fence. I walk parallel to it, balance the box on top of the wire and give it a shove.

It lands in the pile with a faint *whumpf* that I'm ninety per cent sure the guards didn't hear. But it tips onto its side and Chloe tumbles out, the duct tape tearing loose, her arms and legs flopping to the ground like tentacles.

The wires are hard in my fists as I pull myself up. The fence rattles no louder than it would on a windy night. Soon I'm straddling the top, then swinging my leg over as though dismounting from a horse. I drop down on the other side.

No time to stuff Chloe back into the box. Her heels leave trails in the dust as I drag her away from the fence with one arm, holding the box under the other.

Tripwires lattice the ground, showing where walls will some day stand. Concrete obelisks—the foundations—rise above the pebbles and dirt like miniature skyscrapers.

Construction has come a long way since Chloe last saw it. If I'm successful, she'll be sealed under a finished hotel in no time.

In the centre of the site yawns a rectangular pit, deep enough to fit Chloe's whole house. The dirt floor is perfectly flat, ready to have concrete poured into it. This will probably be a basement car park.

I skirt around the edge until I reach the ladder balanced against the side. Then I take one last look around. Neither of the two guards is in view. With the dead body balanced over my shoulder, I descend into the pit.

~

My feet clunk down the rungs, two at a time. Part of me is glad I won't have to carry Chloe back up this ladder. The rest of me is horrified by the callousness of that thought.

I'm about to cover up a murder and spend the rest of my life lying to the victim's family. Whatever ethics I was programmed with, they haven't worked.

Thinking about it makes me feel ill. Maybe the Open AI Community thought the sensation of guilt was good enough.

When I reach the bottom, the floor of the pit looks so smooth that I half expect to disappear into it, like quicksand. But it's tightly packed under my shoes. Digging won't be easy. I walk Chloe and the box over to the middle of the pit.

There are no shovels, but a bucket and a pickaxe lie nearby. The grip of the pickaxe is slippery against my palm. I angle the blade the right way and swing it into the dirt. It punches a neat hole in the ground; narrow, but deep.

I swing again, and a second puncture opens up next to

the first. It takes only a few minutes to make a grid about the size of a coffin.

The bucket works better than I'd expected at scooping out the grit. Now that the ground has been aerated, I can get the lip under the surface and drag out long trenches. After ten scoops, the hole looks wide enough. After forty, it's deep enough. I hope.

I fold the box, drop it into the hole, and roll Chloe's body onto it. Her arms splay out, and I tuck them in by her sides. She hasn't yet started to smell, and the colour is still in her cheeks. She could be asleep.

Just to be sure, I check her pulse again.

Nothing. Her skin is cold as glass.

I pick up the bucket and start pouring the dirt back in. It spatters her knees, her belly, her neck, growing across her like shadows lengthening at sunset.

It's hard to drop dirt on a human face. I look away as I do it.

Smoothing out the silt takes longer than digging the hole. At first I try using the flat side of the pickaxe blade, but it leaves too many grooves and lumps. After a few failed strokes, I get down on all fours and sweep the dirt with my palms, patting it down in places. Soon my hands and knees are black, but looking at the ground, no one would know there was something beneath.

I put the bucket and the pickaxe back where I found them and scan the ground for signs that I was here; footprints, hand prints, scraps of duct tape. There's nothing. I look up at the sky, to see that the clouds have moved on, revealing thousands of glittering stars. The sun won't be rising for at least a couple of . . .

The skinny guard is standing on the edge of the pit, staring at me.

ON THE RUN

'Hey,' the guard says. Then, as if his brain is just catching up: '*Hey!*'

It's over. I'm caught. I'm dead, or will be soon.

A thought flashes through my mind: *In that case, running won't make it any worse.*

I sprint away from the guard. It will take him a while to circle around the pit to the top of the ladder. Maybe I can climb it before he gets there.

Maybe not. My feet pound the dirt.

'Intruder,' the guard yells. 'Ivan, we got an intruder!'

His radio bleeps and hisses. I hear a thud as he jumps down into the pit and dashes towards me. He must have decided that circling around would take too long. Now he's heading right for me—and he's catching up.

His breaths, ragged and fast, get louder. My body refuses to move fast enough to save me.

I throw myself at the ladder, clawing at the rungs. I'm barely three metres up when I feel it wobble. He's climbing after me, right beneath my shoes.

A hand grabs my ankle as I haul myself over the lip of the pit. My battery jolts and, as I shake the hand off, I kick the top of the ladder. The guard yelps and hurls himself clear as the ladder tips over backwards, creaking and rattling, before crashing to the dirt below.

I scramble to my feet and dash away from the pit, weaving through the piles of dirt, racing towards the fence. But the middle-aged guard, Ivan, emerges from the other side of a stack of cement slabs. I duck behind a pile of two-metre long steel rods used to reinforce concrete.

I don't think he saw me, but he's blocking my access to the fence. I can't move unless he does.

The other guard will be propping up the ladder right now. As soon as he comes out of the pit, he'll spot me. I'm trapped.

I can't hear Ivan moving. I peek between the rods, trying to work out where he is.

His stone-grey eyes fix on mine. 'There!' he yells, as he starts to run in my direction. 'Freddie, I got her!'

I grab one of the rods and wrench it out of the stack. Like a baseball player, I take a practice swing. The rod cuts noisily through the air, bending a little.

Ivan stops running, eyes widening. 'Whoa there,' he says, as though calming a horse.

'Stay back,' I yell. The stocking vibrates against my lips.

Ivan looks over my shoulder. I follow his gaze to see the young guard, Freddie, edging towards me.

'Both of you,' I say. But when I turn back to Ivan, he's moved a little closer.

I can't fight them off. Even if I could, I wouldn't. I don't want to hurt them. They're just doing their jobs.

But I can't get caught. My life is at stake.

I bolt sideways, racing towards the corner of the construction site. Both of them give chase immediately—I can hear their boots thudding into the ground. They're gaining on me. But the fence is only fifteen metres away.

Now ten.

Five.

I heave the rod onto my shoulder like a javelin. Then I drive the point downwards.

It digs into the dirt and quivers. I leap into the air, hair smeared across my face, my palms tight around the rod as I catapult myself over the fence like a pole vaulter.

Of course, real pole vaulters have mattresses waiting for them. I hurtle down through an asteroid belt of leaves, sticks crackling and hissing around me, before crash-landing onto a bush.

If I were human, my legs would be broken—but if I were human, I wouldn't be in this mess.

Freddie climbs the fence while Ivan runs back towards the gate. But I have acres of pitch-black forest to disappear in. If they lose sight of me, they won't get it back.

I sprint into the trees, and let the shadows swallow me up.

~

I run for perhaps five minutes before slowing down, worried that the guards will hear me crashing through the forest. I tug the torn stocking off my head, but the darkness is no less smothering.

There are no bus stops or houses around here. Ivan and Freddie will assume I parked nearby. I have to get the car away as soon as possible.

My outstretched hands divert the raking branches as I stumble through the trees. When they can't find me, will the guards realize I was burying something? Will they dig up Chloe's body?

I tell myself they won't. They might not even inform the construction company that there was an intruder. It wouldn't look good on their resumés.

The trees thin out as I approach the road. If I can get to the car before they find it, I'm probably safe.

But when I break through the last of the scrub and find myself on the motorway, two cars are waiting instead of one.

Red and blue lights whirl on the roof of the second vehicle. A police officer stands behind the number plate of Graeme's sedan, tapping on her PDA. She's an oak-skinned woman with narrow hips and neatly pressed trousers. Her hat hides most of her face.

Run, or stay? She sees me before I have time to decide.

'What are you doing?' I bluff.

The policewoman tucks her PDA into her pocket. 'Ma'am, would you like to tell me why you parked here?' The friendliness in her tone is thin.

I jerk a thumb towards the forest. 'I just had to go,' I say, trying to look embarrassed.

Her eyes don't waver from mine. 'I see. Where are you driving to?'

'I'm on my way home from a gig,' I say. Chloe's clarinet isn't in the car, so I add, 'I'm a vocalist.'

She looks at the car, then at me, then at the forest. 'Your parents know you're out here?'

'Sure,' I say. 'Dad lent me his car, but he said he'd call the cops if I wasn't home by three.' My eyes widen. 'Is that why you're here? Am I late?'

'It's two-twenty,' the cop says. 'Where was the concert?'

'Open mic night at the Potbelly,' I say, choosing the pub at random.

'Uh-huh. Got your licence?'

I pull Chloe's wallet out of my pocket, unfold it, and remove her driver's licence. She smiles out of the photo at me before I hand it over. The police officer shines a torch on it and looks at me before handing it back. 'Thanks, Chloe,' she says. 'You mind opening the boot for me?'

Digging out Graeme's keys, I push the button. The lid pops up slightly, and I lift it the rest of the way.

The cop's torch reveals the jump leads, the tyre iron, the duct tape, and a dog-eared road map. 'OK,' she says. 'You can close it.'

It thumps shut and she points back up the motorway. 'Your house is that way. You want to tell me why you're on this side of the road?'

I frown. 'No it's not. To get to my place you have to go up to Antill Street . . .'

'Antill Street is back there.'

'Are you sure?' I sigh. 'I must have missed the exit. Where's the nearest place I can do a U-turn?'

'About a kilometre further along.'

'Great. Thanks.'

She crosses her arms over her chest. I haven't entirely convinced her, but there's nothing she can arrest me for.

'Do a song for me,' she says finally.

I laugh, nervously. 'What?'

'You're a vocalist, right? Sing one of your songs.'

'Here? Now?'

She looks increasingly sceptical. 'You have a problem with that?'

Have I been programmed with the ability to sing in tune? Chloe couldn't.

So I clear my throat, and rap.

'Let me say *hello*, let me *show*, that I *know* you. Tell you *so*, let me *go*, let me *grow* on you. Take a *chance*, take my *hands*, let me *dance* with you . . .'

The cop looks as shocked as I feel. I'm not surprised that I know all the words to this song, since Chloe probably uploaded her mp3 collection into me along with all her e-books, but I'm astonished at how much my voice sounds like a man's. Specifically, that of Chloe's favourite rapper.

I don't have vocal cords—just a speaker at the back of my throat. It can imitate any voice. Perhaps even any sound.

'That's enough,' the cop says.

I've run out of excuses and explanations, so I just stand here.

'Thanks for your cooperation,' she continues. 'Have a nice night.'

'You too,' I say, as she gets back into the police car. She stays seated for a while, fiddling with her PDA again, before pulling out onto the motorway and driving off.

My hands are shaking. Another human handicap, programmed into me for no good reason. The driver's seat creaks under me and I take a few deep breaths—artificial, but they seem to help—before starting the engine and rolling out onto the road.

~

The lights are off at Chloe's parents' house. No voices. No

movement behind the curtains. But the silence and stillness are not as reassuring as they should be.

I park the car exactly where I found it and tiptoe across the lawn. I pull off my shoes, slip the key into the front door as slowly as I can bear, and turn it.

Only shadows greet me on the other side, but I have the unnerving sensation that I'm being observed. Perhaps a hundred people are in here, waiting to shout 'Surprise!' when the lights are switched on.

Perhaps not. I step in and close the door behind me.

Remembering to switch the motion sensor back on, I sneak through the shadows of the house. Still no sign that anyone is here—or that they're not. I pause near Chloe's parents' bedroom and listen.

A rumbling snore. I'm safe.

I'll have to wait until sunrise to wash off the dirt. The hot-water pipes rattle loud enough to wake up not only everyone in this house, but all the neighbours too. In Chloe's room, I collapse onto her bed.

It's over. I evaded Chloe's killers, hid her body, escaped from some security guards, fooled a cop and made it home in one piece. My first day of freedom was a nightmare, but at least I survived.

I pull Chloe's laptop onto my thighs and switch it on. On a local news site, the headlines read: *Government not dependent on PMCs, senator says. Quantum computers soon a reality. Singer caught on camera with new man.*

Nothing about a dead body found at a construction site. But there could be soon, if the security guards called the police.

A widget hovers in the sidebar, listing real-time updates from reporters. A new one flashes up every five minutes.

Capitals falling behind, 18 points to 4. Another aftershock rocks Argentina. Opposition leader says defence spending out of control.

I can't sleep, I know the contents of every book on the shelves, and it's risky to leave the room. There's nothing to do but watch headlines.

Three hours later my head is stuffed with current affairs. But nothing came up about Chloe's body.

Something moves outside the door. Graeme is getting up. I hear him opening and closing the wardrobe, switching on the extractor fan in the bathroom, and turning the tap in the shower. He must be having a cold rinse, since the pipes aren't shaking and groaning.

The water stops three minutes later. His footsteps thud back into his bedroom. I trot up the hall to the bathroom with Chloe's pyjamas bundled under one arm and some jeans and a blouse under the other.

Showering with my new body is weird. No matter how far I twist the taps, I can't get the water hot enough. My skin isn't as sensitive as Chloe's was. My hands stick to my rubber armpits and abdomen. When I wash the dirt off my palms, slivers of soap get trapped in the invisible seams beneath my knuckles. I hang my head and let the lukewarm water tumble down the back of my neck.

I'm not human any more. This is my new life.

When I dry off, the towel leaves thin fibres all over my body. Chloe dressed as a witch for a Halloween party a few years ago, and found similar residue clinging to her prosthetic nose afterwards. I'll have to find a better way to get dry in future. For now, I'll just hope no one comes close enough to see.

Chloe's clothes don't quite fit my shop-window

58

mannequin body. They're a little loose around the thighs and belly, a little tight around the chest and hips. I guess *She's Alive* didn't have a model with her exact physique, so she just went for the closest match. I'll have to go shopping.

But I've only met six people so far, and it's been terrifying each time. How could I survive a shopping centre?

I open the bathroom door to find Graeme standing there. I jolt, then try to cover the movement with a yawn.

'Morning Dad,' I say.

'You're up early,' he says. His voice is deep and rough. It's the first time he's used it today.

'Didn't sleep well. Thought I'd get a head start on the day.'

He nods. 'You want a lift to school?'

Of course. It's Thursday. Am I really ready to fool Chloe's friends and her teachers?

'Actually, I'm not feeling all that well,' I say. I try to breathe only through my mouth as I talk, so my nose will sound blocked, but it doesn't work. My voice sounds healthy as ever. 'I might have to stay home today.'

Graeme frowns. 'That's no good. Symptoms?'

'Sore throat. Headache.'

'Maybe we should take you to the doctor.'

Who would realize I wasn't human. 'Sure,' I say. 'No, wait . . . damn it. I have that test today. For English. I have to go.'

'They'll let you take it some other time,' Graeme says. 'If you're sick, you shouldn't be at school. You could infect somebody.'

'I might not be sick. I might just be tired.'

'Better safe than sorry.'

'I'll see how I feel after breakfast. OK?'

Graeme is a big believer in the healing power of breakfast. 'OK,' he says.

He follows me into the kitchen, where I pour muesli into a bowl and spread dollops of yoghurt across it. Graeme heats the kettle and sprinkles some instant coffee into a mug.

Your digestive system is basically just a plastic tube and a two-litre tank, but it works. I hoped Graeme would leave me alone for a few seconds so I could scrape the muesli into the bin. But he's too close, so I'm forced to trust Chloe.

The first spoonful tastes like wet Styrofoam. It's weird, because my sense of smell is fine, but my tongue doesn't seem to have any taste buds. Chewing works the same way it always did—but swallowing is entirely different. A plughole opens up at the back of my throat and sucks all the air out of my mouth. A valve sprays water against my teeth and cheeks, hosing them down.

'Do you hear that?' Graeme asks.

I wait until the alarming mechanism in my mouth has stopped hissing before I speak. 'Hear what?'

He listens again. 'Nothing. Never mind.'

'Could you put the kettle on again? I'll have a cup too.'

He switches on the kettle, and it overpowers the noise of me swallowing four more spoonfuls of muesli. With practice, the spray can be controlled. I dial it back to a safer volume.

Graeme puts a mug of coffee in front of me. The smell is rich and bitter but, when I take a sip, the liquid has no more flavour than water. The incongruity almost makes me gag.

'How do you feel?' he asks.

'Much better now,' I say, holding up the cup. 'Thanks.'

'So, do you want a ride to school, or not?'

'If you don't mind.'

He takes his keys off the hook. 'We leave in forty-five minutes.'

THURSDAY

I sit on my hands as the car pulls out of the driveway. It's the only way not to fidget.

The road is full of other vehicles, occupied by weary-eyed drivers and passengers who text message or brush their hair.

Graeme drives in silence, one hand knuckled around the gear stick, his gaze motionless on the road.

Is he phrasing and rephrasing a question for me? Or will he wait for Kylie to do it? *Don't you want to know what kind of young woman is living in our house?*

Sometimes the easiest way to deflect a question is to ask one of your own. 'Dad?' I say.

He grunts.

'Do you think defence spending is out of control?'

He glances over at me, surprised. 'Why do you ask?'

I shrug. 'The opposition leader says it is. I heard it on the radio.'

'Well,' Graeme says, 'what they're spending would be fine, if they spent it in-house. But, at the moment, most of it is going to PMCs. That's what I have a problem with.'

'PMCs?'

'Private Military Corporations. Soldiers who work for a company rather than the government.'

'But they *are* working for the government,' I say, 'if that's where the defence budget is going. Right?'

'Not directly. The government hires the PMCs, and the PMCs hire the soldiers, who were often dishonourably discharged from the real military.'

'In that case, why does the government use them?'

'They say it's cheaper,' Graeme says. 'But this year, they've paid more than ever before—a ridiculous amount. And now that the private companies are doing so much R and D . . .'

'R and D?'

'Research and development.'

Sometimes talking to Graeme is like reading assembly instructions.

'They design their own equipment and weaponry, so they can refuse to sell it to defence if they won't hire their soldiers.' His cheeks inflate as his teeth clench behind them. 'The alternative is equipping troops with outdated gear. So the PMCs have a lot of power, without much accountability. That's pretty scary for guys like me.'

'People who work for defence?' I ask.

His voice is filled with quiet anger. 'People who don't think wars should be fought for profit.'

We lapse into silence. A bus trundles past, with almost as many people standing in the aisle as sitting on the seats.

I say, 'Can I put the radio on?'

'Sure.'

I push the button and adjust the volume. A reporter babbles about the weakening dollar and what it means for retailers. When she gets to the headlines, there's still nothing about a corpse found in a construction site. But I can't let myself feel safe. Not until there's a layer of concrete over Chloe's body.

Perhaps not even then. Maybe not until I'm old enough to move out of Graeme and Kylie's place, so as I can live on my own and work from home and never let anyone come near me in case they discover what I am.

And then what? Sit around waiting for my parts to wear out?

Scullin High School is up ahead. We join a long queue of cars, waiting to pull into the drop-off lane.

I stare at the other students. Girls are hugging, boys are punching one another in the arms. Lonely kids are walking with their heads down and their shoulders up. I guess I'll be one of them from now on.

'Chloe.'

Uh-oh. 'Hmm?'

'If something was on your mind,' Graeme says carefully, 'you'd tell me. Wouldn't you?'

'What kind of thing?'

'Any kind of thing. About school, or your friends, or a boy . . .'

Or if I was secretly a machine, say.

I force a laugh. 'I haven't had a boyfriend since I was eight.'

'OK,' he says. 'I'm just saying you don't need to shut me out.'

'I'm not shutting you out.'

Graeme raises a hand, as though surrendering. 'I didn't

say you were. I just want you to know that your mother and I are here for you. Always.'

'I know,' I say.

'When I was a kid,' he says, 'my dad bought me a bike. Dual suspension, twenty-one speeds. I stopped taking the bus and rode it everywhere. One day I went into the super-market to buy a chocolate bar and, by the time I came back out, my bike was gone. The lock was lying on the ground, cut in half. No one nearby had seen anything.

'Dad wasn't the easiest man to talk to. I was afraid he would say it was my fault—I should have bought a stronger bike lock, I shouldn't have spent so long in the supermarket, I shouldn't have been wasting my money on junk food in the first place—so I didn't tell him. I pretended my bike was in our garage and, whenever he invited me to go for a ride with him, I said I had too much homework to do. By the time I'd saved up enough money to buy a replacement, exactly like the one I'd lost, he'd stopped asking.'

This story isn't in Chloe's memories. Perhaps he never told her about it. Maybe she never got the chance to learn about her father, her grandfather and the relationship between the two.

'I grew up dealing with a lot of things on my own.' He looks at me. 'I don't want you to have to live like that.'

My chest hurts. 'I can get out here,' I say. 'Thanks for the lift.'

'No problem,' Graeme replies. 'Can you catch the bus home?'

'Sure. See you tonight.'

I open the door and the noise hits me like a train. Screaming, laughing, shouting. The rattling of thousands of books in hundreds of schoolbags.

I can do this. I *have* to do this.

I get out of the car and wave to Graeme. He nods, swerves out of the queue and disappears up the street.

Hitching Chloe's backpack up, I turn to the school. The grey-brick structure has shuttered windows and thick walls tattooed with faded graffiti. It resembles a prison. Some kids would say it is one.

Students flock towards it all around me. Soon I'll be sitting shoulder-to-shoulder with them in a classroom. Close enough for them to hear my fake breaths and see the knots in my wig.

My hands are semi-transparent in the sun's rays. I can see the faint silhouette of my titanium skeleton. Will this body really fool anyone?

'Hey Chloe,' someone says.

I turn around, but the girl is already moving on. It was a casual greeting, nothing more.

'Morning, Chloe.' Mrs Blatt, Chloe's music teacher, smiles politely and keeps walking.

When Chloe was a little girl, Kylie showed her magic tricks. She'd stuff a handkerchief into her fist and open her palm to show that it had vanished. It took four times for Chloe to see the flesh-coloured pouch taped to the back of her mother's hand but, once she had, it was so bulky and pale that she couldn't believe she hadn't noticed it before.

My new body only looks fake because I know it is. The students and teachers assume I'm made of skin and fat and muscle and bone, so they don't look closely enough to see the truth. I can walk amongst them safely . . .

. . . until they have a reason to be suspicious. Then there will be no going back. Once Chloe saw the pouch, the trick never fooled her again.

~

I know Chloe's locker number and the code to open it, but not where it is. She didn't annotate the map before uploading it to my hard drive. I'm not even sure if this is the right corridor.

The lockers are arranged in ascending order, but that doesn't help much. Many are open, others have students leaning against them, still others are decorated with so many stickers and drawings that it's impossible to read the numbers. Searching for Chloe's locker is like using a street address to find an unfamiliar house in the middle of the night.

This is technically my first day of school, but I have to act like I've done this hundreds of times before. I can't make it obvious that I have no idea where my locker is.

'Chloe!'

Suddenly I'm wrapped up in a bear hug, my face mummified in a girl's curly hair. My plastic throat constricts in terror.

Henrietta. Chloe met her in their first year at school, when the teachers picked them both to publicly welcome a member of the Olympic swimming team who had come to give a speech. 'On behalf of Scullin Primary School,' Henrietta had begun. 'We'd like to thank you,' Chloe had continued. And so on.

After that, they joined forces on all school projects. Teachers started calling them 'the twins' A slow-witted boy once asked if they were real twins, even though Henrietta was taller and had darker skin than Chloe. They had both laughed and giggled and guffawed until they were sent to the principal's office.

She lets me go. Her forehead wrinkles with concern. 'You OK, sweet pea?'

Perhaps she can feel how cold my skin is. 'Sure, Hen,' I say. The name is both familiar and strange. 'Why wouldn't I be?'

Henrietta shrugs. 'I don't know. When you said goodbye yesterday, you seemed like you had something on your mind.'

This observation makes her a better friend than Chloe ever was. Henrietta had been crippled by depression for months last year, not eating, not sleeping yet barely able to get out of bed. But she wore a big smile to school each day, and Chloe never noticed the emptiness behind it. When Henrietta recovered and told her the truth, Chloe thought she was joking.

Yesterday, Chloe would have known that she wouldn't see Henrietta in a while. But she didn't know she was saying goodbye to her oldest friend for ever. Thinking about that makes me want to cry.

'Not that I remember,' I say. I'll probably have to say that a lot. 'Things are good. How are you?'

'We're not done talking about you yet.' Henrietta raises a pierced eyebrow. 'Your parents were out last night, right? You get up to anything fun?'

I picture myself burying Chloe's body. 'Nothing even remotely fun,' I say. 'You?'

'Well,' she says. 'Pete came over.'

Pete is the smug but charismatic captain of the school debating team. He's also the main reason Henrietta joined it. Chloe liked him, but thought Henrietta would make a better captain than he would.

I don't really want to talk about Pete. I want to flee and hide in a toilet cubicle until school is over and everyone has gone home. But I have to act like Chloe would.

'*Reeeaally?*' I say. 'I hope you two crazy kids behaved yourselves.'

She sighs. 'Unfortunately, yes. However . . . ' She elbows my titanium ribs. 'I think he likes me.'

'Duh,' I say. 'He'd be an idiot not to. The question is, is he worthy?'

Henrietta doesn't hesitate. 'Yep.'

I laugh. 'Don't say that! He has to prove his worthiness. Make him bring you a magic broomstick, like in *The Wizard of Oz*.'

Henrietta opens her mouth to say something crude, but the bell rings.

Chloe's best friend doesn't realize that I'm not her. So I take a small risk.

'Hen, my dear,' I say. 'I've completely forgotten where my locker is. Would you care to escort me there?'

She laughs, and links her arm through mine. 'It would be my pleasure.'

~

'Quantum computing,' Mr Fresner says, 'is one of the fastest-growing fields in IT. Who wants to tell me why?'

Silence. Some students don't know, others don't want to admit they do. Chloe uploaded her textbooks into my brain, so I'm pretty sure I know what he's going to say. But I don't want to be noticed.

The classroom smells of formaldehyde and soap. The desks around the walls are fitted with taps that dispense flammable gas to power the Bunsen burners. Chloe heard a rumour that a student once duct-taped the mouth of a dead rat to one of the gas taps. They then inflated it until it burst, showering the room with rat gizzards.

She never worked out whether or not the story was true.

Fresner is a plump man in his late twenties, with prematurely grey whiskers and a habit of pacing while he talks. A faded strip scuffs the linoleum in front of his whiteboard. 'Pete,' he says, undaunted. 'How about you?'

Pete fiddles with a beaded bracelet, which looks like something Henrietta might have made for him. He's a short boy with a mop of black curls and the beginnings of a goatee. He doesn't seem to know the answer, but Chloe never heard him admit to that before.

'Because they can be so much smaller than regular computers,' he guesses. 'Photons are smaller than transistors.'

'That's true,' Fresner says. 'But most of the current designs are about the same size and shape as ordinary processors. And some would argue that computers don't need to be any smaller. You can already fit a pretty powerful one in your pocket. I'll give you a hint—it's something they can do that classical computers can't.'

'Run *Modern Warfare 5* without lagging,' says a boy from up the back.

'Nice try. Next.'

'They're not affected by electromagnetic pulses,' the same boy says, perhaps because no one laughed at his joke.

Fresner pauses. 'Do you know that for sure, or are you just guessing?'

'Guessing,' the boy confesses.

'For those who don't know, an electromagnetic pulse is what happens when you run a current through iron, or another magnetic substance. Any nearby computers will be wiped. It's possible that a quantum computer might not be affected, but I'd have to look it up to be sure. Anyway, it's not what I was thinking of.'

Chloe didn't think to warn me to stay away from magnets. I'll have to add them to the list of things which could expose or kill me.

'They can multi-task,' says the bespectacled girl next to me. 'If you asked a quantum computer to factorize a number, it could try every combination at once instead of going one at a time.'

'Indeed it could. Instead of just using zeros and ones, a quantum computer uses qubits, which are both a zero and a one at the same time until they are measured. So why would that be useful?'

Henrietta is sitting on the other side of me. She puts up her hand. Her rings sparkle in the light from the window.

'Henrietta,' Fresner says.

'Code cracking?' she asks.

'Correct! Where a classical computer might take a thousand years to find a decryption algorithm using trial and error, a quantum computer can try every possibility at once and have the answer in seconds.' He turns to the whiteboard, and writes the word *Cryptography* on it.

I scratch Chloe's notebook with the lid of my pen. Flipping through it told me that the Soviet Union invaded Finland in 1939, that helium is the lightest of the noble gases, and that, in a group of twenty-three people, there is a fifty per cent chance that two or more will share a birthday. It seemed to tell me everything except what I really wanted to know: who was following her, and why?

Her locker held no clues. There was a box of tissues, some photos of her and some friends abseiling down Booroomba Rocks, an invitation to Pete's birthday party which she'd thought was too intricate to throw away afterwards, and a folded note which said, 'Surprise!' and bore a lipstick kiss. Henrietta was fond of slipping quirky letters into Chloe's locker.

'Scientists rarely study things just because they're useful,' Fresner is saying. 'More often, they're researched because they're dangerous. Chloe.'

Everyone turns to look at me. Panic spirals outwards from my chest.

'Yes?' I say.

'Can you think of any reason why a working quantum computer might be dangerous?'

'The world banking network relies on traditional encryption,' I say, quoting the textbook. 'Using a quantum computer, someone could steal trillions of dollars.'

'Well done.' Fresner turns to the rest of the class, who suddenly look more interested. 'In the wrong hands, this technology could create a worldwide economic meltdown which would make the great depression look like a hiccup. This is why countries and companies are racing each other—whoever develops a working quantum computer first will probably also be the first to work out how to protect themselves from such an attack.'

A girl stares at me from the opposite side of the classroom. Her satin black hair is pulled back by a sweatband, revealing a face sprinkled with freckles. Beneath her pointed nose, her thin lips are set in a hard line.

Wondering what she can see that everyone else can't, I

make eye contact with her and smile politely. She doesn't smile back. If anything, she seems to glare for a moment before looking away. Perhaps she's jealous of my textbook knowledge.

I don't recognize her, which means she's not one of Chloe's online friends. But something about her face is mesmerizing. Looking at her makes me feel anxious.

I start writing down bits and pieces of what Fresner is saying. *Cryptography. Bits/qubits. Algorithm.*

Having memorized the textbook, there's not much educational value in what he's saying. The pen seems to move by itself, searching for a more mysterious topic.

Reasons: knowledge, it writes. *Secrets.*

If Chloe had information that someone else needed, that would explain why she was being followed. But she didn't know she had it—otherwise there would be no mystery about the stalking.

She might have passed the knowledge on to me. I just need to figure out why it's important.

My pen scribbles one more word. *Silence.*

What if the stalkers already know the secret? It could be their job to make sure it doesn't get out. Perhaps they planned to kill Chloe all along?

But they don't know they've done it already. So they might kill me for something I don't even know that I know.

My heart is pounding in my chest. Knowing that it's an illusion, that there is nothing but a battery and a two-litre tank in there, doesn't help.

'Something wrong, gorgeous?' Henrietta whispers.

I force a smile. 'No, nothing.'

Yet.

TIGHTROPE

Science feels like it takes all morning, but actually it's only fifty minutes before I'm out. Band rehearsal is next. According to the map in my head, it's on the other side of the campus.

As the last students tumble out of the biology classroom, I grab Henrietta by the elbow.

'Ow!' she says. 'Watch it, Hercules. I need that arm.'

'Sorry,' I say, releasing her. I point to the satin-haired girl who glared at me. 'Who's that?'

'Who's who?'

'Her. With the sweatband and the freckles.'

'That's Becky.'

We both look away as Becky turns towards us. I can't tell if she saw me pointing.

'Is she new?' I ask.

'No, you ditz. She's been in our class all this year—although she took a month off when her brother got sick. Why do you ask?'

'I just don't remember seeing her before, that's all.'

'Wow. What's it like on your planet?'

Be Chloe, I tell myself. 'Come visit some time,' I say. 'I'll show you.'

Henrietta laughs. 'I have to get to Italian. I'll catch you at recess.'

'Ciao,' I say.

'Beg your pardon?' she says, looking confused.

'It's Italian. It means . . . ' Then I realize she's kidding. 'Get out of here.'

She smirks. 'See you.'

Henrietta walks one way, and I walk the other, trying to match the speed of the students around me. Shoulders and hips bump against me as I squeeze through the gaps in the crowd.

It's hard not to feel like everybody is staring at me, no matter how many times I glance around to check. Personal space doesn't exist here. Surely it's only a matter of time before someone touches my skin and recognizes it as silicone.

Then again, I've made it this far.

My music teacher, Mrs Blatt, overtakes me. The grey shawl, the thick glasses, and the suspicious expression on her face make her look a hundred years old, but if she took them off she would probably be revealed as a thirty something. The students move aside uneasily as she passes. I fall into step behind her, the way a gridlocked taxi follows an ambulance.

I'm almost at the band room when an eerie clicking fills the air. It sounds like the noise that earphones make when a text message is sent nearby.

A moment later, I'm horrified to realize that the sound is coming from my own throat.

I clamp my mouth shut and slap my palms over it, trying to muffle the sound. The amplifier in my throat must be malfunctioning. I have to get out of here before someone hears it.

But it's fading, like the ticking of a dog's claws as it trots away down a tiled corridor.

'Are you OK?' someone says. A younger boy, with braces like train tracks across his teeth. No one else takes notice of my strange behaviour.

I let go of my mouth. Will that happen every time someone sends a message near me? Surely not. Henrietta was texting in class, right next to me, and my voice was fine then.

'I'm OK,' I say. 'I just thought I was going to throw up.'

The boy gapes at me. 'Are you pregnant?'

'Who's pregnant?' someone else says.

'Her.'

'Chloe's *pregnant*?' a third voice says.

Everyone's looking at me now.

'I'm not pregnant,' I say, glaring at them all. I'm just . . . I . . .'

Hunching over, I pretend to gag, as though I'm about to vomit on the growing crowd of bystanders. They all scamper backwards, giving me room to push through.

So much for blending in. As I flee, I wonder how many more ways my body can betray me.

~

The ceiling fan in the band room serves only two functions: to throw off our harmonies with a creaking, groaning sound, and to blow our own hot air back down at us.

'Come in, sit down,' Mrs Blatt says as the students shuffle

in. 'Tomorrow's the last day of term, and we still have a lot to get through.' She points her baton at the pianist like a wizard casting a spell. 'Tuning note, please!'

The pianist prods a key. A low B flat rings out across the room. Those who have assembled their instruments join in, fiddling with valves and slides to get the pitch right. The rest weave through the chairs and stands towards their seats.

I'm already sitting, sheet music in front of me, Chloe's clarinet in my hand. My hands are trembling again.

When Chloe wore the motion-capture pads so as I'd know how to move, did she play the clarinet? When I try to play, will my fingers know where to go?

Most of the instruments are tuned. Evidently deciding that this is good enough, Mrs Blatt taps the baton on her stand and waits for silence. A stern look hastens the process.

'Get out *Himalayan Tribute*,' she says.

A few students hiss, 'Yes!' Others groan.

I reach for the music, but the clarinettist next to me—a skinny girl with hair that always seems to be over her eyes—is already pulling out the relevant sheet of paper. She's not one of Chloe's online friends, but she's been tagged in their photographs, so I know her name: Fiona.

I scan the top line of the music. The first few notes are D, G flat, B, A. I can still read music, at least. But can I play it?

Mrs Blatt raises the baton. I put the instrument to my lips, and hold my fingers over what I think are the appropriate valves. Everyone in the room holds their breath.

Mrs Blatt brings the baton down again and sound erupts all around the room. The cymbals crash, the saxophones honk, the flutes trill like birds.

But no noise comes out of my clarinet at all.

Panicking, I blow harder, but nothing happens. The instrument may as well be a lead pipe.

The tune keeps going for another five bars before Mrs Blatt stops the orchestra with a wave of her hand. 'Dynamics, trumpets,' she says. 'There's supposed to be a big diminuendo there.'

'Didn't you practise?' whispers Fiona.

'I did. I think my reed might be broken.'

'Let me see.' She takes my clarinet and inspects the mouthpiece before handing it back. 'It's fine.'

'Again,' Mrs Blatt says, and counts us in.

The first note is deafening, from everybody except me. The clarinet refuses to make any noise—and suddenly I realize why. I can't breathe.

My chest rises and falls, and I can make breathing sounds with the speaker in my throat, but no air is actually moving.

I puff out my cheeks in order to get some pressure, and squeeze the mouthful of air through the instrument. It rattles, and makes an embarrassing squeak, but no actual notes come out.

Mrs Blatt cuts us off again. 'Can I hear just the second clarinets, please?'

That's us. There are no other sounds to hide behind.

Mrs Blatt raises the baton.

A pause.

She drops it. Fiona chimes in, extra loud, but it couldn't be more obvious that she's on her own. Now even my shaking fingers refuse to obey me.

Mrs Blatt cuts us off. 'Chloe . . . ' she begins.

'I'm having some trouble with my reed,' I say.

'That doesn't sound like reed trouble,' she says. 'It sounds like silence.'

Everyone in the room stares at me.

I know what the notes are supposed to sound like, but I have no way of producing them. Chloe spent months assembling my body and brain. Why didn't she realize that this would be a problem?

She would have. And she would have given me a solution.

I fiddle with the reed some more. 'Can I try again?'

Mrs Blatt raises an eyebrow, and wordlessly counts us in.

Putting the clarinet to my lips, I finger the keys as though playing, and a pitch-perfect melody rises through the air. But it's not coming from the instrument. It's coming from the speaker in my throat.

Fiona looks visibly relieved when we make it to the end of the phrase and are cut off. Mrs Blatt stares at me for a moment, probably wondering whether my silence was a peculiar tantrum. But she just turns to the rest of the orchestra and says, 'From the top.'

And then the fire alarm goes off.

As always, a couple of students cheer. As always, several start packing up their instruments. As always, Mrs Blatt shouts at us over the honking of the alarm and the muttering of the students: 'Sit down! All of you!'

This deafening *beep, beep, beep* is designed only to get our attention. We're not supposed to evacuate until the danger has been verified and the sound is replaced by an oscillating siren.

It's rare for a band lesson to get interrupted in this way. The alarm usually goes off during Chloe's history class, which coincides with an irresponsible science class in the year below. They're always looking for opportunities to set things on fire with the Bunsen burners.

Everyone seems to have lost interest in me and the way I couldn't remember how to play the clarinet for a few minutes. Maybe after the alert is over, the incident will be forgotten.

Some kid starts wailing, imitating the evacuation siren. Mrs Blatt opens her mouth to tell him off when the principal's voice comes over the loudspeaker.

'Attention teachers. Please keep the classroom doors shut. Escort your students from the premises via the windows. This should be done in a quick and orderly fashion.'

Her voice wobbles on the last few words. Mrs Blatt stares at the ceiling as the announcement is repeated, baffled and alarmed.

Just what kind of danger are we in?

'OK,' she says, recovering. 'You heard her. Leave your instruments on your chairs. Percussion, you make your way over to the windows first.'

The drummers leave their sticks on their stools and begin sliding back the bolts on the windows.

'Why would they tell us to do that?' Fiona whispers. 'Won't it take us longer to get out of the building that way?'

I nod. 'Maybe a fire started in the corridors rather than one of the rooms.'

She peers at the window in the door. 'I don't see any smoke.'

'Can't smell it either. But it can't be a drill, or they'd take us out the usual way.'

'Low brass,' Mrs Blatt says. 'Follow percussion.'

'We always do,' a trombonist jokes. One of the tuba players laughs, but it sounds forced. They start climbing out of the window into the shrubbery. The percussionists huddle on the grass beyond them, like lost sheep. Groups of students from other classes shamble towards them.

'A bomb threat, maybe,' Fiona says.

'You would think the teachers would want to get us out the quickest way, if that were the case.'

'Maybe the caller said it had to be like this. Part of their demands.'

'Wouldn't the caller tell us not to leave at all?'

Her hands are crushed into fists by her sides. 'I don't like this,' she says.

'Woodwinds,' Mrs Blatt says. 'Your turn.'

Fiona and I follow the saxophonists and the other clarinettists to the windows. Rust lines the frames; they haven't been opened since last summer. Luckily, the school is a one-storey building, but the bushes outside are laced with tiny thorns.

The other musicians didn't complain, so I don't either. I'd rather get a few scrapes than have to stay in here with whatever the danger is.

Just the same, I tell Fiona she can go first. She almost throws herself out of the window, and runs across the oval to join the others. I climb after her, avoiding the prickliest branches, and stumble out onto the grass.

The sunshine highlights my fake skin. I stick my hands in my pockets.

Henrietta is standing on her toes, peering over a group of her classmates. I walk over to her. 'Hey Hen.'

She turns around. 'Hey sweetie. I hear you're pregnant.'

Word travels fast. 'It's triplets,' I say, just as Chloe would have. 'Want to adopt one?'

'Only if its hair matches my furniture. What do you think of the new evacuation route?'

'Way cooler than the old one. And it saved me from a tricky piece of music.'

'It saved *me* from some tough grammar. I don't think I should be forced to learn no Italian until I figure out how to speak English good.'

I chuckle politely.

'I'm going to go find Pete,' Henrietta says. 'OK?'

'Want me to come?'

'Are you going to embarrass me?'

'Absolutely.'

'Then you're staying put, young lady.'

She gives me a hug and trots off into the crowd. I wander over to a group of people and hover near the edge, trying to look like I'm with them.

'It's a gas leak,' one of the boys is saying. 'I overheard Mr Fresner talking about it. He said the sensors picked up chloroflurane in the air, or something like that.'

The rogue science class once left a gas tap running, which could have created a devastating fire if someone hadn't smelled it in time. Afterwards, all the smoke detectors were replaced with chemical sensors, which would sound the alarm if they found any of a thousand dangerous chemicals in the air.

'So the school might *explode?*' someone else says.

'It's not flammable,' the first boy says. 'It's toxic. That's why they wouldn't let us go in the corridor. The gas, like, kills you.'

'You're making that up.'

'I'm not! That's what Mr Fresner said.'

82

'Chloroflurane,' a girl reads off the screen of her phone. 'A halogenated ether historically used for inhalational anaesthesia. Exposure causes unconsciousness in an adult male within two minutes. Permanent brain damage results after twenty-four minutes. Prolonged exposure of forty-five minutes or more causes death.'

'As if anyone would bring that to school,' the first boy says.

'You're making that up,' the other kid says again.

The girl hands him the phone.

'Chloe.' I turn around to see Henrietta wringing her hands. Her dark eyes glisten. 'I can't find Pete.'

I look around. 'They've evacuated the school,' I say. 'He's got to be here.'

'He's not. I've looked everywhere. And I've called his phone. It just rings out.'

Exposure causes unconsciousness within two minutes.

'Hen, you have to tell a teacher,' I say. 'Right now.'

'I already did,' she says. Her face is as colourless as an old photograph. 'But they won't let me go in and look for him. They said there's a gas leak. What do I do?'

The world is starting to spin. I can't think straight. 'The fire department gets called, right?' I say. 'Automatically, when the alarm goes off?'

'But what if they don't get here in time?' Henrietta's voice is almost a whisper, like she's afraid to say the words out loud. 'Last time it took twenty minutes!'

Permanent brain damage results after twenty-four minutes.

It's a big school. How long will it take them to find Pete?

'OK,' I say, grabbing Henrietta by the shoulders. 'Listen to me carefully. I want you to keep ringing Pete. Don't stop for any reason, and don't tell anyone where I've gone. OK?'

'Where *are* you going?'

'I'm going to get Pete. But you can't tell anyone. OK?'

'But . . . the gas . . .'

'Just trust me, OK? Call Pete. Right now.' And I run back towards the school.

RESCUE MISSION

I can't get back into Scullin High the way I came out. A teacher or student will see me and intervene.

Instead, I jog further out onto the oval, circling the school, not close enough that anyone would suspect I'm going back inside. I run slowly, so the movement doesn't draw attention, but still fast enough that I'll be out of view before anyone happens to look over. I hope.

In twenty steps I'll be out of sight. Fifteen. Ten.

Someone shouts, 'Hey!'

Can't tell if they're talking to me. I don't look back. Five steps.

Finally I'm around the corner of the building. The nearest entrance is near the art rooms. I break into a sprint, the wind blustering in my ears.

Through the windows, the school looks as cold and dead as it must on the weekends. But a living thing is in there, somewhere. According to Chloe's watch, I have sixteen minutes to find him.

The door is up ahead. My fingers wrap themselves around the handle.

Even without lungs, I have a sense of smell. Open AI programmed me with human weaknesses—a wobbling voice, shaking hands, the sensation of a heart thumping so hard that it hurts. Could they have programmed me to lose consciousness when I smell the gas, the same as a human would?

Perhaps. But I can't let Pete die out of cowardice. Gritting my teeth, I yank on the door and the air washes over me.

It has a faint odour of wet acrylic paint, which could be the gas or could be art supplies in nearby classrooms. I don't pass out. Perhaps it will take two minutes. I'm not going to stand here waiting to find out.

This corridor contains the lockers for the Year Seven kids. A jungle mural, painted by students who have long since graduated, decorates the walls. Someone has overturned a rubbish bin, spilling snowballs of scrunched-up paper and a slick of chocolate milk across the floor.

I creep down the corridor, listening for Pete's phone. Thanks to the blaring of the alarm, I'm unlikely to hear it from more than twenty or thirty metres away. If it's set to vibrate, I might not find him at all. He'll get brain damage, and I'll have no explanation for abandoning Henrietta.

I have to find him now. Both our lives depend on it.

A faint thud from somewhere nearby.

Could be a window slamming shut in the breeze. Could be Pete, finally losing consciousness—although that should have happened a few minutes ago.

I keep listening, but hear nothing but the siren. I keep walking, peering into every shadow.

Soon I reach a T-intersection. I don't know what class Pete had, so I don't know which part of the school he

86

should have been in. Most of the building is to my left, so I go that way, stepping over the scuff marks in the linoleum.

A drinking fountain protrudes from the wall. The puddle of water beneath it fizzles in some kind of chemical reaction. Something bad is definitely in the air, but I'm unaffected. It can't kill me. I'm no more alive than the paintings on the walls.

Another thud. And another sound—a throat being cleared.

That's Pete's ringtone. He recorded it so he wouldn't have to turn his phone off in class. He must be somewhere nearby.

The doors to the toilets are a little further along the corridor. If Pete had excused himself to go to the bathroom, he might have been caught out in the open when the gas leak happened, and been unable to evacuate with everyone else.

I press my palm against the door to the boys' toilet, surprised by how wrong it feels to go in, even under these circumstances. The door creaks open.

The bathroom looks deserted. The smell—bleach and urine—seems *loud*, somehow. My fake face stares back at me from the grimy mirror.

I walk in, and crouch down to look under the cubicle doors.

Pete is slumped face-down in the second-last cubicle, a pool of blood growing under his head. His nose is twisted sideways, broken when he fell. The whites of his eyes are visible under half-closed lids. His jaw is stretched into a silent gasp, and saliva bubbles like acid around his lips.

I drag him out of the cubicle, roll him onto his back, dig the ringing phone out of his pocket and answer it. 'I found him, Hen. See you soon.'

I hang up before she has the chance to say anything. Eight minutes before Pete gets permanent brain damage. I haul him onto my shoulder. He's heavier than Chloe was. I'm not going to be able to move as quickly. His arms are so long they almost drag on the ground behind me as I stagger out of the bathroom, my forearm locked across the backs of his thighs. I head back towards my science classroom, where the nearest exit is.

When I reach the corridor in which I was accused of being pregnant, the clomping of boots stops me in my tracks.

The fire department must already be here. If they see me, I'll find myself answering difficult questions about how I can breathe. I'll have to avoid them on my way out.

I keep moving, my ears open. A black can of soft drink lies on its side up ahead, hissing. A white spray hangs in the air above it—another chemical reaction. Except . . .

I slow down as I approach. That's not a soft drink can. It has a handle. A trigger. A pin. It's a chemical grenade.

This is no gas leak. This is an attack.

My stomach churns as the footsteps get louder. A dark shape rounds the corner in the distance, followed by three others. Each of them wears a gas mask, but they're not fire fighters. Four pump-action shotguns swivel in their gloved hands.

HUNTED

I duck sideways into one of the classrooms and press my-self against the wall, hoping the four armed men didn't see me.

Their footsteps don't seem to change tempo. I'm safe—unless they come in.

'This is the spot,' a voice says. It's muffled by the gas mask, but filled with testosterone. Deep and aggressive.

'Anybody see a box?' someone else says. 'A bag?'

'No sir.'

My first thought—that this was a terrorist attack—wasn't quite right. They're here to pick something up. But what could be so important that they would attack a high school in the middle of the day?

'OK,' the leader says. 'Fan out. We're on the clock, so do it quick. The package could be in a locker, on top of one, or stuck to the underside of a chair or desk. Report when you've found it.'

'Yes sir.'

The combat boots stomp away in various directions.

The fear feels like a noose around my throat. Whatever 'the package' is, I hope they find it soon. Because if they don't, sooner or later one of them will come looking in here. And I have nothing to defend myself or Pete with. I may be immune to the gas, but one shot from those guns could carve a chunk out of me as big as a bowling ball.

Would I die right away? Or would I be crippled until someone found me and switched off my remains?

There must not have been a class in here when the alarm went off, because the windows on the other side of the room are closed. The hinges look rusty and stiff. Could I open one before they hear me and come running?

Too late. One of the hunters is coming this way.

I could lie next to Pete. They will expect a few sleeping bodies. But the gas is lethal, so they're prepared to kill. If they see two unconscious students, they might finish us off.

Instead, I slink over to the teacher's desk and crouch behind it, but not under it. I tuck Pete's limbs in to keep them out of view.

The door opens. A chair rattles. The hunter is inside.

He comes over to the teacher's desk first. His ammunition pouch jingles as he walks.

I hold my hand over Pete's mouth, momentarily stifling his breaths. The desk bumps and creaks as the hunter reaches beneath it, feeling the underside with his palm.

Apparently satisfied, he moves away. Slowly, carefully, I slide across the floor, keeping the desk between us and him as he walks deeper into the classroom, checking the chairs and tables of the students.

I crawl under the teacher's desk and drag Pete in with me.

We're crammed together so tightly that I can see the fine hairs in his ears.

Furniture rattles. Feet thud. Hands scrape. If the hunter doesn't give up soon, Pete is going to be a vegetable.

The footsteps get closer. Closer still. And then further away as he clomps back out of the door. Moments later, I can hear nothing but the siren.

I crawl out from under the desk, climb to my feet . . .

And see the hunter, still in the doorway. He's facing away from us but, as I duck back down, Pete lets out a phlegmy snore.

The hunter whirls around. His small, bright eyes lock onto mine as he raises the barrel of the shotgun.

I hesitate for a fragment of a second, wondering if I should surrender, watching his finger moving into the trigger guard before I turn, run, *sprint* towards the window, Pete bouncing on my shoulder.

The trigger clicks . . .

The shotgun booms . . .

And the blast hits me in the back like a train.

~

I wake to the sound of angry voices.

'You shot Chloe Zimetski!'

'I didn't know it was her. But she doesn't look hurt, and . . .'

'That's not the point, you idiot!'

Pain. Confusion. I writhe slowly on the ground like a spider sprayed with insecticide. I'm deaf, the microphones in my ears overloaded by the gunshot.

Rolling onto my back, I see the window, cracked from when I hit it. Pete is sprawled on my left. On my right rests

91

a fallen shotgun and a tiny sack of beads. The four hunters huddle around the doorway.

One of Chloe's memories hits me in a rush. Graeme once brought home a 'beanbag round'—a new type of shotgun ammunition which was classified as less-than-lethal rather than non-lethal, since it could rupture internal organs and create fatal internal bleeding.

I have no organs. Other than the pain, the sack of beads left me unharmed.

'We have to bring her in,' one of the hunters says.

I can't let them take me. They'll find out what I am.

I grab the shotgun and climb to my feet.

One of the hunters sees me.

'She's awake, she's awake!' he yells.

Blam! I pull the trigger, and the shotgun lurches in my hands. The discharge hits the hunter's shoulder with the force of a cannonball. He spins like a ballerina before pitching over sideways. Not dead. Not unconscious. But stunned, for now.

I yank the slider. *Chock-chock.* An empty cartridge flies out the side, and a new round slots into the chamber, just in time—the second man is raising his gun. My fake heartbeat is like thunder in my ears.

I pull the trigger. A miss. The beanbag hits the open door, which slams against the wall. I tug on the slider again, frantic. The hunter's own shotgun is lined up with my face. I fire again.

The blast hits him in the gut. Even with the bulletproof vest, it bends him in half. All the air whooshes out of him like a soccer ball under a meat-tenderizing hammer.

Two down. Two to go. *Chock-chock.*

But the other hunters have fled out the door. I barely have time to wonder if I've won before a grenade flies into the room. Different from the last one—it has a set of yellow bands around it, like a bee.

I watch it bounce, once, twice, before reacting. I turn to face the window and pull the trigger.

The cracked glass shatters into hundreds of glimmering pieces. Dropping the gun, I grab Pete and run, launching myself off a chair on my way out.

The frame clips my shin and I yowl as I hit the grass outside, rolling with the impact. Pete lands face-first and stays there. He's going to feel terrible when he wakes up. Henrietta will never forgive me if I've ruined his good looks.

Lightning flashes inside the classroom as the stun grenade goes off with a sound like a thunderclap. Any moment now the remaining hunters will come in and see me through the window.

I haul Pete back up onto my shoulder and run through the wind, trying to get out of the line of fire. Pete's bloody cheek bounces against my hip. No students or teachers are within view. I sprint around the side of the building, hoping the hunters won't shoot me in front of hundreds of witnesses.

Seconds later, the evacuees are in sight. Henrietta spots me coming.

'Pete,' she screams, and starts running.

The whole crowd turns to look at her, and then, following her gaze, at me. I feel horribly exposed.

Henrietta and I meet halfway. I lower Pete to the ground.

'He was just outside one of the exits,' I say. 'He must have inhaled some gas while he was trying to evacuate.'

She doesn't hear the lie. Holding his chin in one hand, she cries his name over and over again.

I look back at the school while a circle forms around us. No sign that I've been followed. That's the second time I've heard them say they want to bring me in. But what does it mean?

Mrs Blatt is the closest teacher. 'People are inside,' I yell at her. 'With gas masks. And guns. I saw them through the windows.'

Her eyes widen. 'Everybody!' she roars. 'Get back! To the far side of the oval! Quick!'

Henrietta ignores her. As the crowd starts to flee around us, she's giving Pete mouth-to-mouth resuscitation, which is silly for two reasons. Firstly, you're only supposed to do that if the victim has actually stopped breathing, which Pete hasn't. Secondly, there's still some toxic gas in his lungs.

'I feel sick,' Henrietta says, her voice slurred. And then she tumbles sideways, sprawling across Pete's body like Juliet over Romeo.

I can't carry two unconscious teenagers to safety—but Mrs Blatt is already picking up Pete. I grab Henrietta under the armpits.

The air seems to shudder.

I turn to the school, searching for the source of the racket. Is it gunfire? More stun grenades? An earthquake?

A helicopter rises from behind the building.

It's a spindly, insectile thing, daubed in matte grey paint. The blades chop the air like a buzz saw. The four hunters are visible through the open door, strapped to the walls inside. Two are clutching their stomachs and shoulders, keeping dislocated bones in place.

One of the others has a rope of tattoos around his neck, which is wider than his head. It takes me a moment to remember where I've seen him before.

He's the man who shot Chloe.

It's hard to tell behind the reflective goggles, but I could swear he's staring right at me . . .

. . . and he's holding an assault rifle.

Apparently witnesses are not an issue. Terrified of being fired upon, I haul Henrietta away from the school as fast as I can, heading for the cover of the trees on the far side of the oval. The screams of the other students drown out the thudding of my feet against the grass as I wait for the air around me to be shredded by gunfire.

But the hunters don't shoot. Whatever their agenda is, a massacre won't advance it. As I look back, I see six fat tyres fixed to the underside of the helicopter. That must be why nobody heard them land—they drove here. By the time the police realize that they need air support, the hunters will be long gone.

The helicopter rises and rises until it's just a fading shadow in the clouds, leaving no sign that it ever existed.

MAKING A STATEMENT

The teachers walk around like sheepdogs, herding the students for roll call. I'm standing near the ambulances while the paramedics examine Henrietta and Pete, who lie on stretchers. They're both conscious now, and it's hard to tell who looks more embarrassed.

'I don't even remember coming outside,' Pete is saying, his voice distorted by the oxygen mask. 'I was in the bathroom . . . and then . . .'

'Memory loss is a pretty common side effect,' says the paramedic, shining a torch in his face. 'Look at the light, please.'

Pete does, his eyes watering. The TV crews zoom in on this from their vantage point outside the school gates. A journalist with painstakingly coiffed hair is on the phone with her production assistant, telling him to go to the hospital with media release forms for Pete and Henrietta to sign. The press already outnumber the teachers and, with more arriving every minute, soon they will outnumber the students.

Terrorists attack high school in the national capital—this will be in the global news cycle for days.

'Is he going to be OK?' Henrietta is asking.

The other paramedic holds her wrist, comparing the speed of her pulse to the ticking of his watch. 'We'll know more once we've run some tests at the hospital,' he says.

'She saved your life, Pete,' I say.

Pete looks at Henrietta. 'Really?'

'No,' she says, and glares at me. 'She's exaggerating.'

'She sucked the poison right out of your lungs,' I continue. 'Gave you the kiss of life.'

'Shut up!' Henrietta hisses. Turning to Pete, she says, 'How are you feeling?'

'I'm fine, really,' he says. I suspect he's just trying to look tough. 'I don't think I even need to go to hospital.'

'Believe me, you do,' says one of the paramedics. 'You look like you fell down a flight of stairs. Come on, off we go.'

Pete disappears as his stretcher is pushed into the back of the ambulance.

'See you at the hospital,' Henrietta calls.

'I'll call ahead and book a bed for two,' I tell her.

She tries to slap me, but I step out of reach just in time. I laugh, and she tries not to.

Then I flinch. For a minute, I completely forgot that Henrietta and I never met before today, and that her real best friend is buried under a construction site.

Is this how it's going to be for the rest of my life? Feeling like I've been kicked in the chest every time I remember who—or what—I am?

Henrietta's face becomes serious, as if she knows what I'm thinking.

'Why did you ask me not to tell anyone where you'd gone?' she asks.

'They would have come looking for me,' I say. 'Then they would've put me back with the rest of the group, instead of letting me find Pete.'

'How did you know you could save him?'

'I *didn't* save him. He was lying outside the door. He would have been fine.'

Henrietta grips my hand. 'I never knew you could be so . . .'

'So?'

'So something. I don't know what.'

I force a smile. 'Thanks, I guess.'

The paramedic starts sliding the stretcher into the ambulance.

'I'll text you when I get home, OK?' she calls.

'Sure thing.'

The paramedic closes the doors, and turns to me. He's a stiff-legged man with the brawny hands of a plumber or a football player. His eyes are colourless beneath a heavy brow.

'I'll need to examine you, too,' he says.

I step back. 'I never went into the school.'

He pulls a wristwatch from the pocket of his scrubs, and holds it up like a hypnotist. 'You went near the doors. You could have been exposed. Don't worry, it'll only take a minute.'

He reaches for my wrist. I snatch my hand away. 'Don't touch me!'

Heads turn towards us. Students. Teachers. Journalists.

'I just want to check your pulse,' the paramedic says quietly, 'and your pupil dilation. It won't hurt.'

'I have my own doctor,' I say. 'I'm seeing her after school.'

There's a pause. He glances over at the media personnel before looking back at me.

'OK,' he says. 'But make sure you tell her everything that happened today. Got that?'

I nod. He climbs into the ambulance and shuts the door. Cameras are raised. Journalists take panning shots of the vehicle as it drives away.

'Excuse me,' a woman with a microphone calls.

I look over at her. 'Yes, you,' she says, beckoning and flashing some perfect teeth. 'Want to be on TV?'

I shake my head and turn away.

'Chloe!' Mr Fresner is waving.

I jog over. 'What's up?'

'You saw the terrorists, right?' he says. Tufts of his hair are poking out from under his cap—he must have pulled it on quickly during the evacuation.

'Just through the window,' I say. 'I didn't get a good look at them.'

'Well, the police would like to ask you some questions.'

'The police? I . . . '

He glances over and I see a familiar policewoman standing nearby. She looks at me, and I look at her.

In any other city, the highway patrol wouldn't be investigating terrorist attacks. But I live in the nation's capital, where the local police are also the federal police. Lucky me.

'Chloe Zimetski,' she says.

'Good memory,' I say. It comes out sounding friendly, I think.

'I'm Detective Anders,' she says, rolling up the sleeves of her ocean-blue windbreaker. 'This is Detective Ericson.'

The other police officer looms like a statue of a politician—larger than life and improbably strong. Under a sunburned nose, his jaw protrudes like the bow of a houseboat. He doesn't look at me. He's staring up at the sky, as though he expects the helicopter to come back down out of it.

'How's the singing going?' Anders asks, in a voice that implies she doesn't expect the truth.

I shrug. 'I haven't done any since you saw me last night.'

Fresner raises his eyebrows at me.

Anders tells him, 'Thanks for your time. We'll call you if we need anything else.'

He nods, and turns back to the milling crowd of students.

Anders brings up something on her PDA. Possibly my address and licence number. 'So,' she says. 'You spoke with the attackers.'

'What? No. I just saw them.'

'But you heard them talking, right?'

Through a window, with the siren going? Not likely. 'No,' I say. 'I only saw them.'

Anders rests one hand on her hip. 'Sorry. I must have misunderstood. Can you tell me what they looked like?'

'They were wearing gas masks, and gloves. All their clothes were black. They all had weapons, too.'

Ericson passes a tablet computer to Anders, who hands it to me. On the screen, a goggled man with a long-distance Taser shoots down a firing range at a target.

'Did they have these?' Anders asks.

I shake my head.

She taps the screen. 'How about these?'

The same man, now wearing ear protection, is taking aim with an enormous tube. I can just make out the words 'weaponized noise cannon' on the side. When he pulls a lever on the top, it emits a shrieking sound like a table saw carving through chains.

'No,' I say, wondering why the cops assume the terrorists had these bizarre weapons. 'They were carrying Remington pump-action shotguns.'

Anders raises an eyebrow. 'You know your guns.'

'My dad works for defence.'

'Does he have a shotgun?'

'I don't think so.'

'Any guns at all?'

'Why are we talking about my dad?'

Anders shrugs, and takes the tablet away. 'Just curious. Were they carrying anything else?'

'Not that I saw.'

Still looking at the sky, Ericson says, 'Grenades?' He talks like Stephen Hawking, with a voice devoid of expression.

The chemical grenade on the floor wouldn't have been visible from any exterior windows. 'Not that I saw,' I say. 'But I didn't get a good look at the equipment on their belts.'

'Any other identifying marks?' Anders asks. 'On their clothing, or their skin?'

'When the helicopter flew away, one of them took off his gas mask and I saw he had tattoos around his neck.'

'What kind of tattoos?'

'I was too far away to see. It was some kind of pattern, dark, and it went from here to here.' I point at spots on my throat.

'How is it that you saw the soldiers and no one else did?'

'I was on the other side of the school. Around there.' I point.

'Where you rescued Peter.'

'Pete. That's right.'

'And you knew he was there because . . . ' She consults her PDA. '"Henrietta" told you?'

'She told me he was missing. I didn't know where he was until I found him.'

'Why didn't Henrietta go looking herself?'

I can feel the net of lies tightening around me.

'You'd have to ask her,' I say. 'She was kind of panicked. Maybe she figured he would be inside, where we couldn't get to him.'

'That seems like a fair assumption. Why did you think differently?'

'I didn't. I just thought I might see him through a window, and be able to direct the fire department when they arrived.'

'And instead you found him on the ground,' Anders says. 'Just outside one of the doors.'

'Right.'

'And you carried him all the way here, to the rest of the group, by yourself?'

Uh oh. 'He's not that heavy,' I say. 'Or maybe it just felt that way, because of the adrenaline.'

'We'll need your number,' Ericson says. 'In case we have to explore more lines of questioning with you.'

I tell them Chloe's mobile number. They already know where I live and where I go to school, so refusing wouldn't do me much good.

'Thanks for your cooperation,' Anders says. 'We'll be in touch.'

They both turn to leave.

'One more thing,' Anders says, turning back. 'I asked the bar staff at the Phoenix. No one remembers your perform-ance last night.'

I fight to keep my expression neutral. Would she really have done that?

No. It's a test.

'I wasn't at the Phoenix,' I say. 'I was at the Potbelly.'

'That explains it,' she says, without a hint of surprise. 'Thanks again.'

They disappear into the crowd, muttering to each other. Perhaps they're talking about me. Perhaps they just want me to think they are.

~

The principal announces that the school won't be safe until the gas dissipates in six to ten hours. Now that the roll has been checked, we're supposed to spend the rest of the afternoon studying at home. Judging by her expression, she knows that this will be interpreted as permission to take the day off.

'I can't stop you from talking to the media,' she adds, 'but I would strongly discourage it. Until we know exactly what happened here, anything you say is likely to be misleading, and I'd rather none of you looked foolish on national TV.' She leans forward. 'Think of how *embarrassing* that would be.'

Fear of embarrassment is a powerful incentive. Short of telling the kids their hair or make-up was a mess, this warning is more effective than anything else she could have said. Duly chastened, the students leave without re-sponding to the cries of the press. Some younger kids get on the phone to call their parents. Others bounce towards the bus stop, bickering about which shopping centre to go to and which fast food chain to gorge themselves at when they arrive. Already the attack is on its way towards being forgotten.

Senior students head for the car park, drivers fiddling with keys, passengers calling 'shotgun'. Fiona loiters with two flautists.

'Hey Chloe,' she calls. 'We're going to the cinema. Want to come?'

Avoid social engagements when you can, but when you can't, be friendly.

'Sorry,' I say. 'Doctor's appointment at four-thirty. Don't think I'd make it back soon enough.'

Fiona's eyebrows ascend. Perhaps she heard the pregnancy rumour.

'OK,' she says. 'Next time.'

'Next time the school gets attacked by terrorists?'

'I was thinking public holidays,' she says, 'but whatever. See you.'

'Bye.'

They trot away towards Fiona's car, and I'm left wondering what I'll do with the rest of the afternoon.

Being at Chloe's school, going through her locker, meeting her friends and teachers—none of this helped me understand why she was targeted, or by whom. I've thoroughly inspected her room, but now that her parents are both at work, it might be a good opportunity to search the rest of her house.

I walk towards the road, where a school bus is already squeaking and hissing to a stop. I join the queue, and pull Chloe's MyWay bus card out of her wallet while I wait.

Only now do I notice how empty the wallet is; no receipts, no photos, no loyalty cards for coffee shops or scraps of paper with reminders scrawled on them. Just a bank card, a library card, and a drivers' licence.

It's as though it's been sanitized to hinder my investigation. Or perhaps her life was as empty as mine.

I climb into the bus, tap the MyWay against the sensor pad, wait for the beep, and look around for a seat. I find one next to a girl who's talking on her phone and is unlikely to pay me much attention.

As I tuck Chloe's bag behind my feet, I notice Becky, the freckled girl from science class. She presses her ticket against the machine and, when it beeps, she turns around and sees me.

She glares for a split second. Then she walks past without looking at me, and sits near the back of the bus. The boys on the seats behind her nudge one another and laugh in a predatory way, and I realize she's very pretty, or would be if she smiled. She hangs her head, letting her dark bangs tumble across her face.

'Oh my God.' The girl next to me is still on the phone. 'You would not *believe* the day I've had.'

I know how she feels.

~

The bus lets me out at one end of Chloe's street and, as the doors groan and it rolls away from the kerb, I start walking all the way to the other.

I move quickly. The hunters talked about 'bringing me in'. I'm not safe until I'm inside Graeme's fortified house.

The windows of the homes give me snapshots of the occupants' lives as I trudge past. An old man paints his living

105

room wall the same colour it was before. A woman gyrates on an exercise machine, shining with sweat, eyes locked to the TV. A ragamuffin cat stares at me from its perch on a windowsill. When the wind changes, I smell sausage rolls from the bakery at the local shops.

I tug some mail out of Chloe's letterbox and check the return addresses as I walk up the driveway. Something from a telephone company, and something from Graeme's sister, who lives in Borneo. Something intended for the previous owners, who still get letters every month despite having moved to the other side of the country more than twenty years ago.

I unlock the door, push it open, and drop Chloe's schoolbag just behind it. This feels like something I've done a thousand times, even though it's never happened before; at least, not to me. I'm living in a state of endless déjà vu.

In the last few weeks of her life, Chloe spent most of her time in the basement, building me. If I want to figure out what she didn't know she knew, that might be the best place to start.

The stairs creak as I descend. My birthplace doesn't seem to have been disturbed in the last twenty-four hours. I bundle up the nylon net and put it in a box, along with the TV and the cables. Then I slide the box into the darkness beneath the workbench, as though it hasn't been touched in years. If Graeme goes looking for evidence of Chloe's project, he won't find much.

The drawers are filled with hardware supplies—nails, screws, and cubes of chalk like the ones used to polish pool cues. One drawer is full of motherboards, processors, and other computer parts. This might be where Chloe got the components of my brain. There are so many bits and bobs in here that Kylie would never notice if some went missing.

I turn to the computer itself. I already know she used it to control me when I was first switched on, and presumably to modify my programming before that. Perhaps she kept an electronic journal.

I switch on the computer, and find that it's password-protected—which seems promising, since her laptop wasn't. I try Chloe's email password, and it works.

The computer's hard drive is almost full, since it has the equivalent of a human brain stored on it. The folders are named after neurological functions: short-term memory, long-term memory, hand-eye coordination, imagination, language, and so on. I read through the whole list, but there's nothing marked *What I know about the people following me*.

I open up a search field and type *stalker*. Only one result turns up, and it's the dictionary definition of the word, stored within a sub-folder labelled *vocabulary*.

The front door slams up above. I look up, surprised. Graeme and Kylie don't usually arrive home until after six.

'Thanks for coming,' It's Graeme's voice.

'No problem,' says another voice. Female, soft—and not Kylie's. 'It wasn't hard to get away.'

Unsure of what I'm hearing, I rise to my feet and creep up the stairs. The basement door is thick, but not enough.

'I had to see you.' Graeme's voice is an urgent whisper. 'My daughter's school was attacked.'

'Attacked? By whom?'

'People with guns, chemical grenades, and a land-to-air vehicle.'

There's a pause. And then my flesh crawls as the woman speaks.

'You don't know it was them,' she says. 'Even if it was, it couldn't have had anything to do with you.'

INVESTIGATION

The wood of the basement door is cold against my ear. I can hear Graeme and the woman talking clearly, but it doesn't help me understand. How could he be connected to the men who killed his daughter?

'You're telling me it's a coincidence?' Graeme hisses. 'No. You'll have to do better than that.'

Footsteps. They're moving away from the front door.

'Look,' the woman says, still within earshot. 'They don't know I'm the one who took the QMP. Even if they did, they couldn't possibly know I gave it to you. Unless you told somebody?'

'Nobody. Do you think I'm an idiot?'

A pause.

'Hey!'

'Well, what do you want me to think?' the woman demands. 'You don't trust my bosses with the QMP. Fine. Neither do I. But you don't trust *your* bosses with it either, and you won't destroy it.'

'*Destroy* it? It's a huge breakthrough. It's revolutionary. I can't . . .'

'Well, how long do you plan to keep doing nothing?'

'I'm trying,' Graeme hisses, 'to work out who they're leaning on in the defence department. How can I risk giving the QMP to anyone until I'm sure?'

I don't recognize the acronym. QMP could stand for a million things. What are they talking about? That's the Question Most Pertinent if I want to Qualify My Problem and Quickly Make Progress.

'If you haven't told anybody you have it,' the woman is saying, 'then they can't be targeting your daughter. If it was them who attacked her school—and I'm not saying it was—then there must have been another reason.'

But they *are* targeting me. They were stalking the real Chloe, before they killed her.

'These are ruthless people. You said they'd pay a fortune to get the QMP back.'

'They would.'

Graeme says, 'Doesn't it also stand to reason that they'd be willing to kidnap Chloe?'

'Willing? Yes. Able? No. Like I said, they don't know you're involved.'

'You said they have sources inside the police force.'

'Graeme, trust me. No one knows you have it.'

He says, 'If they grab my daughter for revenge . . .'

'Don't be stupid. These people don't care about anything except money. That's what makes us better than them. If they grabbed your daughter, it would be for ransom—but if they knew about you at all, they would have taken her from here instead.'

'Then why attack the school? What were they trying to do?'

She sighs. 'I'll do some digging at work. If it was them, there'll be some trace of it. OK?'

'It *was* them.'

'Well, I'll look. There's nothing more I can do.'

'You'll let me know,' Graeme says, 'as soon you find anything?'

'Of course. We're in this together.'

'Sure we are. Now that you've dragged me into it.'

'We're doing the right thing, and you know it,' the woman replies. 'The defence minister herself is clean.'

'You know that for sure?'

'I'm positive.'

Graeme sighs. 'OK. I'll get the QMP to her within the next forty-eight hours.'

'Good. I have to go, or they'll get suspicious.'

Footsteps clatter back up the hall towards the front door.

'Call me,' Graeme says, as the door squeaks open.

'You got it.'

The front door closes. Shoes crunch away across the garden path. Silence, then; perhaps Graeme is watching through the peephole, checking that she isn't being followed. Maybe he's just thinking.

Then he starts moving again. His footsteps get closer and closer to the basement door.

A jolt of fear zips down my spine. I tiptoe back down the stairs as quickly as I dare. There's nowhere to hide down here, so I sit down in front of the computer. Some headphones are tangled up in the cables under the desk. I pull them free and jam them over my ears.

The basement door creaks open. Without looking up, I bob my head as though listening to music.

'Chloe,' Graeme says. I ignore him. It's not until he's almost at the bottom of the stairs that I look up at him, and jump in my chair.

'Dad!' I say. 'You nearly gave me a heart attack.'

'You're home early,' he says, cautiously.

So is he, but I don't say so. 'School was cancelled. There was a gas leak—well, at first they said it was a gas leak, but actually it was terrorists! Everyone's fine though, don't worry.'

'Are you serious?'

'Yep. Terrorists released a knock-out gas in the school, but everyone made it out safely. There was one kid who got dosed, and Henrietta inhaled some of it when she was giving him mouth-to-mouth, so they both had to go to hospital—but they were both conscious before they got put in the ambulances. She's going to text me when she gets out.'

Graeme puts a hand on my shoulder and squeezes the silicone. 'But are *you* OK?'

I smile. 'Relax, Dad. It wasn't even that scary, since I kind of thought it was a drill until they let us go home afterwards.'

'Did the police catch them?'

'Not that I know of. They escaped in a helicopter.' Trying to sound natural, I ask, 'Can you think of any reason terrorists would choose my school?'

Graeme shakes his head. 'Since they didn't kill anyone, it doesn't sound like terrorists at all.'

'What does it sound like?'

He bends down and kisses the top of my head. I try not to flinch. 'Don't worry about it,' he says. 'We'll know more soon enough. I'm just glad you're OK.' He looks at the screen over my shoulder. 'What's this?'

'Science homework. Neurology.'

'That's pretty advanced. When I was in high school, we never learned anything more specific than biology.'

I shrug. 'The other students are studying proteins. I wanted to go a bit more in-depth.'

He chuckles. 'Why does that not surprise me?'

I turn back to the computer and try to look like I'm studying. He opens one of the drawers beside me, and frowns.

'What are you looking for?' I ask.

'I . . . I bought some parts at the hardware store a few weeks ago, and left them down here.' He rummages through the drawer with growing urgency. 'Have you moved anything?'

No, but Chloe might have. 'Uh, I don't think so.'

He stares at me. His gaze is unbearably intense.

'You're not sure?' he asks.

'I'm pretty sure. What are you missing?'

I can see the anxiety in his face, but clearly he doesn't want to tell me exactly what's going on. He pulls open another drawer. Digs through the contents. Slams it closed and steps back, dragging his hands through his thinning hair.

'Dad?' I say. 'What's wrong.'

'Nothing,' he mutters. 'It's nothing.' The veins stand out in his neck. His hands are squeezed into fists.

Electrical pulses zip through the wires that make up my brain. Metallic synapses fire.

I'm not happy she's started spending all her time in the basement.

What if the QMP, whatever it is, was hidden down here? What if someone broke into our house earlier today and stole it? What if the attack on the school was just a distraction?

The theory doesn't quite make sense—Graeme would still be at work right now if it weren't for the attack. I'd still be at school. And the hunters clearly believed they were searching for something there.

But I'm getting closer to the truth. I must be.

~

Kylie comes home while Graeme is stir-frying some vegetables and rice for our dinner. 'Chloe!' she cries, as she comes through the door. 'Are you OK?'

I'm sitting on the couch and scribbling in my school notebook, the same way Chloe used to. The words are all possible motivations for the hunters—*blackmail*, *espionage*, *revenge*—but above them I've written *Themes in Hamlet* in case someone finds it.

Not that there's much risk, since I don't know anything worth putting to paper. I've worked out that the mystery woman stole a QMP from her employer and gave it to Graeme, who was supposed to pass it on to someone in defence, but didn't trust them to have it. He kept it here at the house, and it has since vanished. The woman's employer then sent soldiers to search for it at Scullin High School— the same soldiers who were following Chloe.

But why were they stalking her? Who are they? Why did they think the QMP would be at the school? And what *is* a QMP, anyway?

My head is filled with so many questions that it might burst.

Kylie stares at me. I haven't answered her question.

'I'm fine, Mum,' I say. 'How are you?'

'I heard what happened at school,' she says, dropping her handbag onto a chair. 'They didn't hurt you?'

'I'm fine. They never even got near me.'

She takes my hand and squeezes it, making me nervous. My hands feel like the least realistic parts of me—soft, rubbery things that occasionally bend in the wrong directions. But Kylie doesn't seem to notice.

'If anything like that ever happens again, you run,' she says. 'You run as fast as your legs can carry you. Got it?'

'I *did* run. And I'm fine. See? Lesson learned.'

'Do you want to take next week off school?' she says. 'Are you traumatized?'

'Thanks Mum, but for the millionth time, I'm fine.'

Graeme ladles the food into three bowls and two microwave-safe containers, and we all sit down at the table to eat. Chopsticks feel alien in my hands—perhaps I was never programmed with that skill—so I use a spoon. No one comments.

Kylie asks endless questions about the attack on the school. She's more thorough than the cops were. Her voice covers the hissing and sucking of my mouth as I swallow the food. When replying, I find myself embellishing the tale, describing my desperate search around the outside of the school, the lifeless way Pete was sprawled on the asphalt, how heavy he was when I carried him. If I can't be honest, at least I can be entertaining, and I feel a strange need for Kylie to be proud of me.

But I wish I could tell the truth to someone.

Graeme stares into space, saying almost nothing. His lips are swollen from chewing on them. When prompted, he tells us his day was 'tiring', but offers no more information. I was hoping for clues to identify the woman who paid him a visit, but he gives me nothing to work with.

When the conversation dries up, I stop eating, and carry my bowl over to the sink.

'Thanks, Dad,' I say. 'That was yummy.'

'You're finished?' he says. 'Already?'

'Yep.'

'You've been eating less and less lately. You're not starving yourself, are you?'

I gesture at my body, which is slightly curvier than Chloe's was. 'Do I look like I'm wasting away?'

'Well,' he says, embarrassed. 'There's more in the fridge if you get hungry again later.'

'Cool.'

I wash my bowl and spoon, dry them, and stack them in the cupboards.

'Night Mum,' I say. 'Night Dad.'

'You're going to bed?' Kylie asks. 'It's only . . . '

'Homework, study, you know. I've got a test tomorrow.'

'I thought your test was today,' Graeme said.

'Postponed due to terrorism.'

'Oh. Well, study hard.'

I go to the bathroom to empty my food tank—the process, thankfully, seems to work the same way for me as it does for humans—before washing my hands, walking into Chloe's room and shutting the door. One day down. I hope tomorrow is easier.

I do have studying to do, but not for school. I can't get the freckled girl with the silky hair out of my head. Who is Becky? What's her problem with me? And why didn't Chloe think it was worth warning me?

Becky's number isn't in Chloe's phone. I switch on Chloe's laptop, and go to a social networking site. Becky is not on Chloe's list of friends. But because I know her age and her school, it doesn't take long to find her profile.

Her full name is Becky Lieu. Most of the activity on her page is cryptic status updates and in-jokes I don't get, although there are a few conversations Chloe's friends participated in:

Becky: *Is it cool if I'm a little late to the party? I have basketball training after school, and I'm going to have to bus home to get my costume afterwards. The timing's a bit tight.*

Pete: *Sure thing. You bringing anyone?*

Becky: *I was kind of assuming you'd provide the guests.*

Fiona has left a comment on one of Becky's older posts:

Becky: *You told me grief came from things left unsaid. But I thanked you for everything you did. I apologized for everything I did. There was nothing left to say, and still it feels like you pulled my heart right out. It's been two hundred days. I still miss you.*

Fiona: *I'm so sorry, Becky. We all think about him. Call me if you want to talk.*

Henrietta said Becky took a month off when her brother got sick. I guess he didn't recover.

A few people have posted photographs of Becky. She's at a restaurant, pulling a face—googly-eyed, lips puckered—perhaps because the photographer told her to smile. Now she's sitting under a tree at the school with her legs crossed at the ankles, feet bare, watching the girls' soccer team as she eats a kiwi fruit with a spoon. There's something about her face that makes her easy to spot, even in the background. Another picture has her in the foreground, grinning at the camera with her arm wrapped around Pete's neck and a soft drink in her hand. Henrietta is standing nearby, agony in her eyes, although the embrace doesn't strike me as romantic.

But what would I know about romance? I don't have a heart.

A hundred photos later, I haven't learned anything worth knowing. Becky is a mystery—a girl on the periphery of Chloe's social life whose brother passed away recently, who plays basketball, eats fruit, makes cheesy faces in photographs and who never seemed to actually cross her path.

I almost don't see what I'm looking for when it appears. It's another photo from Pete's birthday party. Becky doesn't seem to be in it, so I click *next*—then my brain catches up with my eyes and I click *back*. In the foreground, a boy has lifted his Iron Man mask over his head to take a sip from his drink. In the background, people dance, laugh, dig in bowls of chips.

Outside the window, Becky and Chloe stand on the porch. Chloe is saying something, her brow furrowed, while Becky listens intently.

I zoom in, staring at the picture. But even the world's best lip-reader couldn't pluck a sentence from a photograph.

Besides the hostility Becky radiates every time she sees me, this is the only evidence I've found that they knew each other. So what did they talk about? And why did they have to do it out of everyone else's earshot?

~

Most computers have a sleep mode. I don't.

I lie on my back, the sheets bunched around my ankles, watching moonlight quiver on the walls as the curtains flutter. The bed doesn't feel as cosy as it used to. My shoulders and calves are cold. My body doesn't generate any heat to get trapped under the blanket.

Kylie taught Chloe a trick for when she couldn't sleep.

She would pick a three digit number at random and try to divide it by a two digit number. If she got to three decimal places, she'd start again with different figures. The task was boring, exhausting, and absorbing—the perfect combination to drain consciousness away.

It doesn't work for me. The numbers come instantly. 127 divided by 31 equals 4.096774193548387 recurring. The precision of this computation freaks me out, so I stop.

But I'm human enough to hate doing nothing. Chloe never sat down to watch TV. She had it on in the background while she tidied the living room. On the bus to school, she annotated her study notes. Even while she was jogging, she would play the clarinet in her head. When she found herself doing a dull chore, she phoned Henrietta, put her on speaker phone, and listened to her while she did it. Unfortunately, neither Henrietta nor her parents would respond well to a call this late . . .

Phone calls.

Emails and text messages can be intercepted, so Graeme probably phoned the woman today, to tell her to visit the house. A cautious man would block his caller ID. A very cautious man would delete the call record afterwards.

Is Graeme quite that careful? Maybe not. By looking up recent calls, perhaps I can find the woman's number.

I sit up. Graeme and Kylie have gone to bed. Our phone only stores the last fifteen calls, so I need to check the number before it's erased.

I open Chloe's bedroom door and stare into the darkness. Shapes become brighter, dimmer, blurrier, sharper, as my video processing unit automatically adjusts the contrast. Nothing moves in the shadows.

The carpet squishes under my bare feet as I slip into the living area. The luminous buttons on the telephone are reflected in the TV screen. I pick up the handset and scroll through the last-dialled numbers. Every beep seems deafening, but there are two walls between me and Chloe's sleeping parents. If they open their door, I should have time to put the phone back in its slot before they see me. I can pretend I'm getting a glass of water—because that went *so* well last time.

Only two calls were made today, both after the woman came to visit. Maybe Graeme deleted the number after all.

Or maybe he called her from his mobile. He wasn't here, after all. They arrived together.

Right now, his phone is as far away from him as it will ever get: on the charger beside his bed.

I creep back towards their bedroom. Put my hand on the door handle. Try to work up the courage to turn it, and fail.

What would be my excuse? If they wake up and find me in their room in the middle of the night, what could I possibly say?

Tomorrow morning. When he's in the shower, making enough noise to cover me. That's when I'll get it.

I release the door handle, and tiptoe back to Chloe's room, shutting the door behind me. I lie on the bed, stare at the ceiling, and wait for a sandman who will never visit again.

FRIDAY

The shuddering pipes interrupt my troubled thoughts. Graeme is in the shower.

I scramble out of bed and walk swiftly up the corridor to Chloe's parents' room. Their door is slightly ajar. Graeme must have left it that way when he went to the bathroom.

I peek through the gap. One of Kylie's feet sticks out from under the blanket, cocooned in a woollen sock, toes pointed to the floor. She's asleep, face down.

I drop into a crouch and push the door quickly to avoid squeaks. When the space is wide enough to slip through, I move towards Graeme's bedside table on my hands and knees. A cable is attached to the power board under the bed. I follow it up to the phone, grab it, and tap the screen.

It's locked, with a PIN. I try Kylie's birthday. It works.

Kylie snuffles against the pillow, and the slats creak under the bed. I freeze. Listen.

No more sound. Not waking up—just rolling over.

According to the log, Graeme made four outbound calls yesterday. One was after the woman's visit. Two were before the school was attacked. The remaining one was to a local landline and lasted only two minutes.

I memorize the number, and lock Graeme's phone again.

The shower stops running.

He must be in a hurry. I don't have time to escape from the bedroom before he comes back. So I jam the phone back into the charger and roll under the bed, where I lie perfectly still.

The door creaks open. Graeme's bare feet—calloused heels, hairy toes—thump across the floor towards the bedside table. Keys jangle. A wallet snaps closed. The phone is lifted out of sight.

A few seconds later, the feet thud over to the wardrobe. One of them disappears, and then reappears in a thin black sock. Alarmed, I turn my head.

Graeme's shoes are under the bed with me.

The other foot disappears, and doesn't return. Graeme must be having trouble with the sock.

I pinch the shoes between my fingers and lift them. Carry them over until the toes protrude slightly from under the edge of the bed. Gently lower them back down.

Graeme's other foot returns, toes wiggling in the sock. Both feet turn to face the shoes.

I stare at them, willing his knees not to bend.

They don't. He stoops rather than crouches, and I see a flash of clipped nails and a silver-plated wristwatch before the shoes are pulled out of sight.

Kylie mumbles something.

Graeme says, 'What?'

'Have a good day at work,' Kylie says, her voice muffled by the pillow.

'You too.' A pause. 'You should get up soon.'

'Uhhmf.'

His shoes laced and tightened, Graeme leaves the room.

Kylie's awake, but not yet up. It would be safer to wait until she's left the room before I come out from under the bed. But I don't know how long that will take.

I'm still deliberating when I hear a knocking from elsewhere in the house.

'Chloe?' Another knock. 'Do you want a lift to school?'

Uh oh. He's at my door.

'Are you awake?'

I grit my teeth, willing him not to go in.

The handle squeaks. The hinges groan.

A pause.

Graeme's feet pad back down the corridor, to the other end of the house.

'Chloe?'

It's not a big house. I might have time to slip out from under the bed before he comes back. I might not.

I don't. Graeme's rapid footsteps thump back up the corridor. The door swings open again.

'I can't find Chloe!'

Graeme sounds frantic, but Kylie barely sounds awake. 'What?'

'She's not in her room. I'm calling the police.'

'*What?* Hang on.' Kylie shifts in the bed above me. 'She's probably just in the bathroom.'

'I was just in there,' Graeme cries. 'She . . . '

'Calm down. Is the car still out front?'

'I'll check.' Graeme leaves again.

I wonder how long it'll take them to look under the bed.

Kylie's feet are already on the floor. She's muttering under her breath, mostly panicked-sounding swear words. It would probably come as little consolation that her daughter is already dead, and can come to no further harm.

She stands, grabs a dressing gown and stumbles out of the room.

I crawl out from under the bed and stand behind the door, listening. This is an impossible situation. If they find me in the house, what's my excuse for not responding to them? If they find me outside, what's my excuse for leaving the house?

I could pretend to have slept through the yelling. But I don't know how thoroughly Graeme searched Chloe's bedroom. Can he be absolutely certain I'm not in bed?

'Chloe?' Kylie calls. Damn—it sounds like she's in Chloe's room now.

Graeme is shouting, 'Chloe!' His voice comes through the window. He's in the back yard, leaving me with a clear path to the front door.

I crawl out from under the bed and poke my head out the door. Kylie is out of sight within Chloe's room. I creep down the corridor, into the living area. Past the laundry and the basement. Towards the front door.

'Chloe?' Graeme is coming back in. The yard is small—it didn't take him long to check it.

I grab the handle, yank the door open and step out onto the front porch. Trot down the stairs, hit the driveway, and then . . .

'Chloe!'

I turn around. Graeme is on the porch, staring at me.

'Hi Dad,' I say. 'Do you smell something burning?'

Kylie appears behind him. 'What are you doing out here?' she demands.

'The smell woke me up. Smoke. Can't you smell that?'

The lie tumbles from my mouth with sickening ease. Like dogs, Chloe's parents turn their faces to the sky and sniff.

'No,' Kylie says.

I pretend to smell the air. 'Oh. It's gone now.'

Graeme hugs me fiercely. 'You scared the heck out of me. Out of us.'

'Sorry, Dad.'

He lets go of me and takes a deep breath. We all go inside together. The mystery woman's phone number is branded on my electronic brain.

~

Swear words, clumsy drawings, accusations scratched into the paint. Like most bus stops, the bench is decorated like the walls of a lunatic asylum. Perhaps all human beings are one long wait away from madness.

The bus lumbers up the street towards me like a fat, herbivorous dinosaur. I hold out Chloe's MyWay card. The brakes squawk.

The door hisses open and I climb on, nodding to the driver and tapping the sensor. The driver closes the door without looking at me. Her face is framed by knots of steel wool hair and enormous black glasses. I know from Chloe's memories that some of the other students are often rude to her, and that she compensates by ignoring all of us. Perhaps she pretends she's driving a completely empty bus around the town.

Only one seat is free—next to Becky.

My hands curl into fists in my pockets. What is more likely to expose me? Sitting next to a girl who has an unknown, unpleasant history with Chloe, or refusing to sit next to her in front of so many of my classmates?

I sit down, accidentally rubbing the skin of my arm against hers. 'Hi,' I say.

Becky shifts in her seat, turning to face the window.

The boys on the seats behind us are babbling about a game that's just been released. The ones on the seats in front have headphones over their ears. Becky and I have some privacy. But what can I say? What will help me figure out what she and Chloe talked about at Pete's party?

'I'm sorry, OK?' I say.

She turns to look at me. Her eyes are as still as those of a waxwork. 'You're sorry?'

'Yeah. I wasn't thinking.'

Lips pulling back over white teeth, she says, 'You weren't *thinking?*'

Whatever Chloe did, it was something really bad. 'I'm sorry. What can I do to make it right?'

'It's six weeks too late to do anything.' She looks out of the window again.

Six weeks. That's how long it's been since Pete's party.

I had assumed this wasn't personal. Looks like I was wrong. Could this be about Becky's boyfriend, maybe? Did Chloe get too close to him?

Reflected in the grimy glass, I can see tears in her eyes. My instinct is to hug her, but she might push me away, which could catch the notice of some of the other passengers. So I do nothing. I sit in silence beside the crying girl, waiting for my stop to arrive.

When it does, I join the queue of students shuffling off the bus and step out into the daylight. Unable to convince myself that the sunshine doesn't make me look fake, I head for the school at a fast jog. A boy in the entrance is raising money for diabetes research. Most people are dropping coins into his donation box, so I do too.

My first class is science. I have all the books I need, so I can skip the lockers—this gives me time to make a quick phone call.

I don't want to use Chloe's mobile, even withholding the number. The call is safest if it comes from someone who has nothing to do with Graeme. So I go to the pay phone in the school cafeteria, which gets used hundreds of times per day by kids who've had their mobiles confiscated.

I dial one-eight-three-one to block the caller ID, and then punch in the number from Graeme's call log.

It rings twice.

'Thanks for calling Ares Security. You're speaking with Nadine.'

Her voice gives me chills. It's definitely the woman who came to the house with Graeme.

'Can I speak to Sam Fletcher?' I ask, choosing the name at random.

'I'm sorry, I don't know anybody by that name.'

'Have I called the wrong office?' I repeat the woman's number, with one digit changed.

Through the glass doors, I can see Becky passing the boy with the donation box. She takes all the cash out of her wallet—at least eighty dollars—and pushes it through the slot. He beams at her, but she walks away without smiling back.

'Sorry,' Nadine is saying. 'This is five *three* double four.'

'I see. Have a good day.'

I hang up. Nadine, from Ares Security. What's her connection to Graeme? And what does Ares Security do?

Questions spin through my head as I walk to science class. I arrive without having found any answers.

'Morning, Chloe,' Mr Fresner says as I walk in.

'Good morning, sir.'

I'm the first here. I flop down into my chair and wait for the others.

'I hope you've recovered from yesterday's excitement?'

'Yes sir.'

'Good. I'm very glad that Pete is OK but, next time, you should tell a teacher what's going on.'

Henrietta had told a teacher Pete was missing, and they did nothing. But I can't see any advantage in arguing about this. 'Understood, sir.'

'Good.'

The other students are filing in and taking their seats. Fresner says, 'OK everybody, we pick up where we left off yesterday. Who can tell me where the world's most powerful quantum mechanical processor was built?'

'University of Bristol,' someone says.

'Correct. And how powerful was it?'

'Not very,' says the girl next to me.

A little laughter. Across the room from me, Becky is digging her fingernails into her desk.

'Also correct,' Fresner says. 'It managed to find the prime factors of twenty-one, but that's something you should all be able to do in your heads.'

Stop. Rewind.

Quantum Mechanical Processor.

You said they'd pay a fortune to get the QMP back.

~

I can feel my mouth falling open as everything swims into focus.

Ares Security. Private Military Corporations. Soldiers who work for a company rather than for the government.

Ares Security built a quantum computer. One that could do more than just factorize twenty-one. In the wrong hands, this technology could create a worldwide financial meltdown which would make the great depression look like a hiccup.

Nadine must have decided that the hands of Ares Security were the wrong ones. But Graeme didn't want the defence department to have it either. No wonder—this technology could turn the whole world upside down.

And now, assuming I'm right about Graeme's frantic search of the basement, it's missing.

'Sir, can I go to the bathroom?' Becky is saying.

'Sure,' Fresner replies. As she gets up, he says, 'Who can tell me what Shor's Algorithm is?'

The girl next to me raises her hand. I watch Becky leave the classroom. She still looks distressed, and suddenly I wonder where she's really going.

Does she know something about the QMP? Is that what she and Chloe talked about at Pete's birthday party?

Becky is the piece that doesn't fit. A link to the most elusive part of Chloe's life.

I try to replicate a sound from a TV show Graeme was watching last night. An old man in a hospital bed, coughing and wheezing.

What comes out of my mouth is a rattling, choking, phlegm-drenched sound. Everyone stares at me.

'Can I get some water?' I rasp.

'Go,' Fresner says, immediately. I run out of the door and follow Becky, turning Chloe's phone off as I go.

Trailing someone on foot is harder than I expected. The school corridors are deserted except for Becky and me, so there are no other sounds to cover my footsteps. But I can't slow down. Every time she turns a corner, I risk losing her.

She's moving cautiously. She ducks below the window in each classroom door as she passes by.

But she hasn't done anything incriminating yet. The bathroom is this way. If she passes it, I'll know for sure that she's up to something.

Becky's hair, carefully plaited today, bounces as she walks. Her arms are crossed as though cradling a newborn baby.

The bathroom doors come up on her left. She walks past the boys', where I found Pete. Then she takes a final glance around and pushes open the door to the girls' before slipping inside, leaving me to decide whether or not to follow.

If she's making a phone call, I want to hear it. But it was difficult to come this far without being spotted, and it will be even harder in there. Less space, more mirrors.

She clearly wants privacy, so she will be in a cubicle. It all depends on how quietly I can open the bathroom door.

I put my palm flat on the door and give it a gentle push, wondering why bathroom doors are always so much heavier than regular ones. But it doesn't creak. I put my fingers between the door and the frame to stop it from banging closed, and then step all the way into the bathroom.

To find Becky staring at me.

'What are you doing?' she demands.

'What are *you* doing?' I reply, without thinking. Tears are pouring down her cheeks. Her chin is dimpled like orange peel.

'I asked first,' she hisses.

I step forward. 'Look, I'm—'

'Don't come near me.'

I stand still, baffled. My toes are curled up inside my shoes. 'I care. Tell me what's going on.'

She looks at me like I've just stabbed her in the heart. 'You know full well what's going on.'

'Pretend I don't,' I say. 'Tell me how I can help.'

'You lied,' she says. Her voice is a choking rasp. 'You said you needed me.'

'I do need you,' I say, with no idea what she's talking about.

'That kiss meant nothing to you,' she sobs.

I think back to the photo. Becky and Chloe, having a serious conversation on Pete's verandah.

How could Chloe leave this out?

Why didn't she tell me that she was in love?

THE SECRET

'You ignore me for six weeks,' Becky cries, 'and this morning you say you're *sorry?*' Her whole body quivers with misery and rage. The rawness of her pain fills the room. I'm drowning in it.

Dozens of excuses whirl through my head. *My parents wouldn't let me see you. I fell down some stairs right after the party and lost my memory of it. My uncle died and I couldn't think about anything else.*

She won't be convinced by any of those. But I can't let her go on believing her girlfriend betrayed her. She looks like she's already on the verge of madness. I don't want to push her over the edge.

'It's not what you think,' I say.

'You used me.' The agony in Becky's eyes is unbearable. 'I was an experiment for you, and you threw me away like I was nothing.'

'Chloe Zimetski is dead.'

The words slip from my mouth, unbidden. I freeze, as though complete stillness will stop her from hearing what I just said.

Becky makes a short, mirthless laugh. 'Have you lost your mind?'

I could pretend to be joking. I could act like she misheard me.

But it wouldn't work. There are too many signs that I'm artificial. To suspect what I am is to see it. My only hope is to get her on my side.

'I'm her replacement,' I say quietly. 'I'm a machine.'

'Just how dumb do you . . .'

I start unscrewing my forearm from the elbow joint. Becky's eyes widen with horror as my wrist turns around, and around, and around. Then, as my arm pops off, she screams.

I drop the arm, step forwards and clamp my other hand over her mouth. Her brown, terrified eyes are inches from mine.

'I know this is scary,' I say. 'But please be quiet.'

'*Mmmmmf!*' Her breath is warm on my palm. She tries to pull away, but I follow, pushing as she pulls, until her back is pressed against the wall.

'*Mmmf!*' she says again. '*MMMF!*'

'Please stop. Someone will hear us.'

Her eyes are rolling back. Her lids flutter. She's going to faint. Maybe from the shock, maybe because she's spent too much oxygen screaming and isn't getting enough through her nose.

I let go of her mouth just in time to grab her armpit as she slides down the wall, unconscious. I lower her to the floor and check her pulse. It's weak, but who am I to judge? Leaning over her face, I listen. She's breathing.

I pick my arm up off the floor, thinking that if anyone came in and saw it my secret would be out. Then I remember that it already is.

As I screw it back into position, I look at Becky. The eyelids and cheeks and lips of Chloe's secret girlfriend. She's very beautiful. I can see how Chloe fell for her—but I don't know why she didn't tell me.

I rest my face in my hands. I never properly mourned Chloe. I was too busy trying to cover up her death, and since I had her looks and memories, in a way it didn't feel like she was gone.

But now a deep, dry well has opened up in my chest. Chloe loved, and was loved. Her death subtracted something meaningful from the world, something that's gone for ever.

I'm a poor substitute for her. No hormones, no pulse. Did the Open AI Community even give me the capacity to love?

Becky's eyes open. Her pupils shrink as she stares at me.

'I need you to stay quiet, OK?' I say.

She says nothing for a long moment. Then, 'What are you?'

It takes a few minutes to tell her the story of my life. How I woke up believing myself to be Chloe Zimetski, only to watch the real Chloe die. How I had to hide her body, because taking over her identity was my only hope of staying alive. How the terrorists who attacked the school were actually employees of Ares Security, searching for a quantum computer that was stolen by Nadine, given to Graeme Zimetski and has since gone missing.

Rivers of tears cascade down Becky's cheeks as I speak. When I'm done, she starts thumping the back of her head against the wall.

'No,' she says. 'No, no, no!'

'I'm sorry. But it's the truth.' I pull a sheet of paper towel from a dispenser and pass it to her.

'Why didn't she tell me she was being followed?' Becky asks. 'Why didn't she tell you about me?'

'I don't know.'

She wipes away the tears.

'Yes, you do,' she says finally. 'She was ashamed of me.'

'No, she wasn't.'

'She must have been.'

'At Pete's party,' I say, 'did she seem ashamed?'

'Maybe.'

'No, she didn't.' I think of the note in Chloe's locker. The lipstick kiss. *Surprise!* 'It was you who left that note in her locker, wasn't it? The day after. You wouldn't have done that if you thought she was embarrassed by you.'

'It doesn't matter what I thought at the time. Afterwards, she ignored me for six weeks.'

'Chloe's father stole something from some very dangerous people. The sort of people who'd gas a school in broad daylight and shoot a teenage girl.' The chronology is coming together in my head. 'After the party, but before you next saw her—that's when she must have realized they were after her. If she didn't want to put you in danger, she would have stayed away.'

'You can't prove any of this,' Becky mutters.

'No. So here's the big question.' I look her in the eye. 'Are you going to help me?'

'*Help* you?'

'We can't get the soldiers arrested for Chloe's murder,' I say. 'Not without getting me killed. But we can prove that they attacked the school. Then they'll be locked up for that.'

'Whether the killer is jailed or not, Chloe . . . Chloe will still be . . . '

'Yes,' I say, before she has a chance to start crying again. 'And I can't promise that you'll feel better after getting the soldiers caught. But if we don't try, it's only a matter of time before they hurt someone else.'

Becky rests her head back against the wall. Thinking.

'Please,' I say. 'I can't do this on my own.'

There's a hardness in Becky's zircon eyes. 'OK,' she says. 'I'll help you.'

It's been almost fifteen minutes since we left science. Becky goes back to class first, since Fresner might be suspicious if we return together. I wait a minute before following her through the school once again.

My secret is too heavy carry alone. It's a huge relief to have shared it with someone. But the comfort is offset by new stresses. Becky is smart, but unstable—only minutes ago she was a trembling wreck. Can she be trusted not to tell anybody?

A thought freezes me in my tracks. What if she's telling the whole science class, now that I'm not there to stop her? They'll think she's crazy, at first. But then, when I walk in, they'll take a closer look . . .

Get a grip, I tell myself. She wants justice for what happened to Chloe, and I'm her best chance of making that happen.

Just the same, my footsteps are slow and heavy towards the classroom door.

When I open it, everyone is staring at me, shock and revulsion in their eyes. I stare at Becky, who looks away.

She told.

~

'Chloe?' Mr Fresner says. 'Are you OK?'

I look at him, and see only concern in his features. No suspicion. Of course—my over-the-top coughing fit. That's why everyone's staring.

'Yes sir,' I say. 'Just choked on some dust. Sorry.'

I take my seat. He resumes his spiel about photons and measurement and logic gates, and I listen. Now that I know Ares Security is looking for a Quantum Mechanical Processor, this just became my favourite class.

Why were they searching for it here? That's the thing that confuses me most. They built it, Nadine stole it, and then she gave it to Graeme. At what point could it have wound up at Scullin High?

Chloe could have found it and brought it here—but why? And why wouldn't I have those memories?

I've done all I can with the facts I have. Now I need new facts. The four men who attacked the school—I know what they look like, and I know who they work for. With Becky's help, maybe I can find them again.

But I have no idea what to do after that. If I go to the police, and they catch the soldiers who attacked the school, three out of the four will say that I shot them. This would lead to some difficult questions about how I was walking around inside the school while it was full of toxic gas. And other than going to the police, I don't know how to find out why Ares was after Chloe.

One step at a time, I guess. Track down the guys first. Then decide what to do about them.

Tomorrow is Saturday. The first day of the school holidays. I wonder if Ares Security operatives work on weekends.

The bell rings.

'Thanks for your hard work this year,' Mr Fresner says, raising his voice over the closing of books and dragging of chairs. 'Don't lose too many brain cells over the holidays. Remember, most neurons don't grow back.'

With that, we tromp out into the corridor. Some of us will be in Mr Fresner's class again next year. Most won't. It's a shame that Henrietta isn't here to say goodbye—he was her favourite teacher.

Becky and I part ways without making eye contact. She looks more stable. I tell myself it's not an act. But she's just found out that her girlfriend is dead, and she can't tell anyone—her mental state probably isn't good.

Henrietta told Chloe that depression felt like wearing leg irons under her clothes, made all the more exhausting by her compulsion to conceal them. She recovered with a combination of medication and Cognitive Behavioural Therapy, which I don't know much about.

I text her as I walk to my next class. *Hey Hen. How's the hospital? I was wondering if you could give me some tips on CBT. A friend needs help.*

She will probably think the friend is a fabrication, and that it's me who is depressed. It might be easier to let her think that than to explain about Becky.

The rest of the day whirls by in a blur of roll calls and lazy farewells. Now that the exams are over, many teachers play Blu-rays instead of trying to educate us. Each class is only an hour long, so by the end of the day I've seen the first half of five different films. The last one is forgettable Oscar-bait and, after the first few dreary minutes, I start fiddling with Chloe's phone under my desk.

An online search for Ares Security brings up a few news articles. *PMCs deny excessive force allegations. Intelligence leak linked to Ares.* In both cases, no charges were ever laid. The company seems to have an army of lawyers which makes it untouchable.

Their official website is politely unhelpful. No phone number, no email address, no physical location. A photo of Warren Christiansen, the CEO, beams alongside a brief history of the company. His greying hair is neatly trimmed, his slightly tubby midsection is constrained by a dark pin-stripe suit. His face looks soft—all except his eyes.

Apparently Ares specializes in robotics and artificial in-telligence, which means they'll see right through my fragile disguise. I'll have to stay well away from them.

Other pages contain contact forms and information about the company's 'ongoing support' for various environmental and humanitarian charities.

A text arrives from Henrietta. *Hospital sucks. They'll kick me out soon—I've eaten all their egg-salad sandwiches. CBT is about getting rid of thought patterns which lead to negative emo-tions. I have lots of tips. Everything OK, sweetie?*

Becky's having a rough few weeks. Some negative thoughts are inevitable. I type, *Everything's fine. I'll pick your brain about it later.*

When the message is sent, I look up Ares on a stock exchange website. It's not listed amongst the other mili-tary corporations, but another one catches my eye—Hera Global. It's by far the biggest private military corporation on the index.

Henrietta once called Chloe 'Hera'. Probably one of her ancient Greek figures.

I look it up. Hera was the goddess of women and marriage . . . and the mother of Ares. Bingo.

Searching for information about Hera Global, I discover that it's the parent company of Ares Security. It doesn't seem to own any other corporations, or provide any services of its own. Warren Christiansen is the majority shareholder.

A shell corporation. Maybe Ares are tax cheats as well as murderers.

Unlike Ares, Hera does have a listed business address. It's less than fifteen kilometres from here.

What if I could get a photograph of Chloe's killer entering or leaving the building?

I send Becky a quick text under the desk. *Got a lead. Busy this afternoon?*

The reply appears in seconds. *Nothing I can't cancel.*

The last bell rings and the Blu-ray gets ejected, half-watched. I say farewell to Chloe's friends and wish them a nice summer before going back to her locker to empty it.

Five minutes later I'm on the cracked concrete in front of the school. The wind tears at my wig, threatening to pull it off.

It'll take half an hour to ride the bus to Hera Global and forty-five minutes to get to Chloe's house afterwards. Add thirty minutes for snooping, and I'll get home about ten minutes after Graeme does. Therefore I need a cover story.

I dial his mobile. He picks up after two rings.

'Hi Chloe.'

'Hi Dad, how are you?'

'I'm fine. Everything OK?' He sounds worried.

'Everything's good,' I say. 'Just wanted to let you know that I'm going to stop by the hospital to visit Henrietta this afternoon, so I'll be a little late.'

'OK. You need a lift afterwards?'

'Thanks, but I'll be all right.'

'You sure?' Graeme says. 'It's no trouble.'

'I'm getting a lift with Becky.'

'Have I met Becky?'

'Uh, don't think so,' I say. 'She's a school friend.'

'What's her last name?'

'Lieu. L-I-E-U.'

'What's her phone number?'

'Relax, Dad.'

'I'm relaxed. I just want you to be safe.'

'I'll text it to you,' I say. 'OK?'

'OK. See you tonight, honey.'

'See you.' I hang up.

'Was that your dad?'

I turn around to see Becky hovering behind me, her bag slung over one shoulder.

'Technically,' I say, 'no.'

She doesn't laugh. 'Oh, right. Sorry.' She walks towards one of the school buses, which trembles as the waiting engine purrs.

'Not that one.' I point to a different bus. 'We're going this way.'

She nods, and follows me. We join the line of students, shuffling towards the passenger door.

'What are you going to do?' she asks. 'Long term?'

No one seems to be listening, but I try to keep my answer non-specific. It's not hard. 'I don't know. I'm not sure there is a long term.'

We both tap our passes against the sensor, trudge to the back of the bus, and sit side by side. It's awkward, somehow, sitting this close to Becky while wearing her girlfriend's face.

'Because you think it'll end?' she says. 'Soon?'

It sounds like we're talking about a relationship, rather than my eventual discovery and subsequent death. 'It can't last for ever.'

'That sucks. I'm really sorry.'

'Yeah.' I say. 'Me too.'

We fall silent. The unavoidable truth—that some day I will be in pieces while Graeme and Kylie weep for their daughter—is hard to face.

'Maybe I can help.'

'How?' The word sounds more desperate than I intended.

'The things you can't do,' Becky says. 'I'll tell people I saw you doing them. Like, spitting, or whatever.'

I smile. 'I can spit. But thank you. That's a good idea.'

She's adjusted to the situation with impressive speed. Earlier today she thought she was being given the cold shoulder by her girlfriend. Now she's already started to feel sympathy for Chloe's mechanical ghost—a sympathy Chloe herself said no one would feel.

'I see why she liked you,' I say.

Becky looks down at her hands, squeezed between her knees, and says nothing.

~

The buildings get taller and the entrances grander as the bus weaves towards the town centre. When we pass the thick walls of the old prison, I hit the stop button. 'We're close,' I tell Becky.

The bus stops and we clamber off. The crowd of pedestrians flows around us like river water around stones.

'Which way?' Becky asks.

I point. 'Hera Global owns Ares Security. Their headquarters are around that corner.'

We thread a path through the horde of shoppers and businesspeople. I'm not as nervous as I was at the school, but it's still hard to shake off the feeling that someone is about to stare at me, point a finger, and scream.

No one does. We turn the corner and find ourselves looking at the head office of Hera Global—a shimmering glass spike, windows polished so highly that I can only see reflections of the other buildings around it. One side of the building is slightly sloped, making a sharp wedge at the distant summit. The only sign is the street number, eleven. Nothing indicates who works there or what they do.

I start to cross the road, hoping for a closer look, but Becky grabs my upper arm. 'Above the doorway,' she says.

It takes me a moment to see the door—a pair of recessed glass panels which presumably slide aside when approached. Two CCTV cameras wait above it in tinted plastic bubbles.

'Anyone who walks past gets recorded,' says Becky. 'They could recognize you.'

I nod. 'That café over there could give us a better angle when the doors open.'

'Let's go.'

We walk into the café, and approach the counter. The walls, scratched and brown, are decorated with 'coffee facts' of dubious validity. *Fact: toffee is made by mixing tea with coffee!*

We buy two hot chocolates from a sullen barista and sit at a table outside. My chair wobbles on a leg which is slightly too short.

'Can you drink?' Becky asks.

'Yes,' I say. 'But I can't taste it.'

'Do you remember how it's supposed to taste?'

I think about it. 'Yeah. Chloe must have put that memory in. Or the Open AI contributors did. There's a lot in my head, but I don't know where most of it came from.'

'That's called source amnesia,' Becky says. 'Your brain considers the information itself more important than where you got it, so the recollection of learning it just disappears. It happens to everyone.'

That actually makes me feel better. 'Thanks.'

'You're welcome.'

We stare across the street at the glass tower, waiting for the doors to open.

'Do you have a plan?' Becky asks.

'Sort of,' I say. 'Chloe's murderer was at the school—I recognized his tattoos. If I can get a picture of him entering or leaving the building, then I can take it to the police. I'll say I recognized him on the street and followed him here.'

'But he saw you inside the school, somehow breathing the toxic gas,' Becky says. 'If he's caught, won't he expose you to the cops?'

'I don't know,' I say. 'I hope not.'

'Maybe there's another way. If we can get access to their email records, we could send all the data we find to the police anonymously.'

'We'd need someone's password, wouldn't we?'

Someone is approaching the front door of the building. A middle-aged woman with red hair, pulling a roller-suitcase behind her. Becky whips out her phone and takes a picture.

'Evidence,' she says.

She takes another picture as the automatic doors open, revealing a receptionist behind a desk and two broad-shouldered security guards with guns holstered on their hips. They nod to the woman as she walks in. The doors slide shut behind her.

'Cameras *and* guards,' I say. 'Even if we got that email password, we couldn't get inside to use it.'

'Maybe we wouldn't have to. Most companies have off-site backup servers and password recovery tools.'

I raise my eyebrows. 'You think you can break into their systems?'

'I think *we* can. You were—Chloe was teaching me programming. That's how we first got to know one another.' She looks like she might cry, but just as I'm about to try to distract her, she takes a deep breath and keeps talking. 'Did you inherit her IT skills?'

'I'm not sure.' I can picture myself using a command prompt, but I don't know if this is knowledge or imagination. 'Either way, we'd need to find the backup servers, somehow.'

'Any ideas?'

'No.'

We stare into our hot chocolates for a moment. I haven't touched mine. Becky's is still three-quarters full.

'We could hire a private investigator,' she says. 'Tell them we know Ares Security is responsible for the attack on the school, and get them to find the proof.'

I shake my head. 'They wouldn't take a pair of teenage girls seriously. Even if they did, they might find out that Chloe is dead.'

'Chloe is dead,' Becky repeats. Her voice wobbles.

'Sorry,' I say. I've had three days to get used to this, but she's had only a few hours. I place my hand over hers. Her skin is warm.

She shuts her eyes. 'I can't believe she's gone.'

'I know. I wish things were different.'

'If things were different,' she says, 'you wouldn't exist.'

Can I be glad that I'm alive and at the same time wish Chloe was? I can't change the situation, so it doesn't seem to matter.

The strangest thing is how stern and cold Chloe seemed when I met her. What did Becky see in her?

'I don't know you,' I say, 'and you only know a version of me. But if you want to talk about Chloe, I'll listen.'

'Talking won't do any good,' she sniffles.

'It can't hurt,' I say. 'We can help each other. You need to tell someone how you feel, and I need . . . ' I hesitate. What *do* I need? ' . . . to understand who I was supposed to be.'

Becky looks up at the sky, tears brimming in her eyes. Then she frowns.

'The top of the building isn't flat,' she says.

It slopes up to a long edge, like the blade of a chisel. 'So?'

She wipes her cheeks with a napkin. 'So where's the helicopter they attacked the school with?'

'It had wheels,' I say. 'They must have landed it somewhere before they came back.'

'And just left it in a car park somewhere? With all the cops looking for it?'

'No, they would have . . . ' Finally it hits me. 'There's another way in. For cars.'

'I bet Chloe's killer didn't use the front door,' Becky says. 'Let's go look.'

We leave the café, cross the street and skirt around the building. It's wide, but not so deep. It doesn't take us long to walk the perimeter. An alleyway is concealed behind, shaded by the towers on either side. It's only just broad enough for a rubbish truck to drive in and empty the skip bins.

When Becky and I walk through the alley, no cameras are visible. I suppose they could be hacked, or recordings stolen. If company operatives come here after illegal jobs like the one at the school, it makes sense for them not to create more evidence than they have to.

A heavy roller door looms behind the bins about halfway up the alley. Big enough for the helicopter to drive through. No keyhole, but an intercom is bolted into the wall. This probably means company cars don't have remote controls to open it. Bad luck for us.

The door for pedestrians has no handle. It looks like it only opens from the inside. A fire door, perhaps.

'Not a good stake-out spot,' Becky says. 'We'd have to wait at one end of the alley. And at that distance a phone camera won't do any good. We'll need something with a telephoto lens.'

'Plus, we don't know which way the tattooed guy will come in.' I watch the distant traffic whirring past on the main street. 'If we choose the wrong end, we'll only get photos of the back of his head.'

'So we'd need two cameras. One at either end.'

The thought of cradling a camera alone on the street for hours and hours, waiting for the tattooed man, gives me a sinking feeling.

'Kylie has a pretty decent camera,' I say. 'She . . . '

A black sedan enters the far end of the alley.

I drag Becky behind the skip bins and listen to the approaching tyres, my scalp tingling with fear. The alley has no other entrances, so the roller door is the car's only possible destination. The driver must be an employee of Ares Security.

The car cruises past and turns. Suddenly Becky and I are sandwiched between the skip bins and the passenger-side door of the sedan. The glossy paint reflects our terrified faces back at us. I press my back against the bin, trying to stay out of the wing mirror.

The intercom beeps as the driver pushes the button. 'Powdered wood,' it crackles.

'Stitches new,' the driver replies.

His voice is familiar. Very, very slowly, I raise my head to peer in the window. It's one of the operatives who attacked the school, but not the one who shot Chloe. The bruises under his chin probably came from hitting the floor after I shot him with a beanbag round.

He's alone in the car. Perhaps the other three guys are already inside. Or perhaps they're out on other missions. Attacking other schools, perhaps.

Becky looks questioningly at me. I drop back down and nod, confirming her suspicions.

She gets out her phone, opens the camera app, and hands it over. I raise it above my head, hoping she's turned off the sound, and push the button.

The phone silently takes a picture. I hit the button twice more, in case the first photo is too blurry, and then snatch my hand out of view.

'Status?' says the intercom.

'Successful.'

'Passengers?'

'One.'

I didn't see any passengers. He must mean himself.

The roller door clanks and starts sliding upwards. The driver revs the engine a few times as he waits.

Thump.

I look at Becky. Her eyes are wide. She heard it too.

Thump, thump. A groan.

I look at the boot of the car. I can't see it rattling, but that's definitely where the noise is coming from. Ares already has their next victim.

The wheels crunch against the asphalt as the car starts to move.

Becky can see what I'm thinking. She shakes her head wildly.

Ignoring her, I crawl out from behind the bins and fall into step behind the car, crouching as I run. The sedan rolls through the door into the darkness and I slip in behind it.

I glance back in time to glimpse Becky's horrified face before the roller door slams shut again, sealing me inside the headquarters of Ares Security.

INCURSION

The car park is surprisingly cavernous, with what looks like too few pillars to support the massive weight of the building above. The sedan rolls down a ramp with me scampering behind it before bouncing over a speed bump and cruising past a mostly empty row of parking spaces.

The ones that aren't empty are occupied by military vehicles. A hulking armoured personnel carrier. A utility vehicle with a belt-fed machine gun mounted on the back. A collection of remote-controlled bomb-disposal robots and unmanned aerial drones. Weaponized noise cannons, like the one I saw in Detective Anders' video, are stacked up against the wall.

Does this mean Anders already suspects Ares? I hope so. But there's no time to think about that right now.

A helicopter with wheels is crouched at the far end of the car park, doors open. This is more than evidence. This is proof.

I keep running behind the car, head and shoulders down. I fumble with the boot, looking for a button or a latch.

There's nothing. Just a keyhole.

More thumping and groaning from inside. It sounds like the prisoner is wide awake, but gagged.

I dig into my pocket, pull out the key to Graeme's car and jam it into the lock. It won't turn.

Desperate now, I twist as hard as I can, hoping to break the lock. But it's hard to apply much pressure while the car is moving.

The car purrs up to a set of steel doors and stops. I brace myself and turn the key with even more force. The metal creaks, but doesn't snap.

The doors slide open to reveal a giant lift, designed for heavy cargo. A CCTV camera hangs from the ceiling.

I can't go in. The camera will see me, and then I'll have to deal with a building full of well-armed soldiers who know exactly where I am.

The car eases towards the lift. Following behind it, I try to wrench the key out of the lock, but it's stuck. At the last second, I give up and dive aside, leaving the car to roll into the lift with the key protruding from the boot, like part of a clockwork toy.

With my back pressed against the wall outside, I strain my ears for some indication that the driver saw me in his wing mirror. My counterfeit heartbeat thumps.

The car door opens. Footsteps clop towards the lift door.

I sprint over to the nearest pillar and stand behind it, listening.

The driver doesn't follow. I hear him push a button and, as I peer around the edge of the pillar, he steps out from between the closing lift doors. The car, and its mysterious passenger, are going up unescorted.

Without looking around, the driver strolls through the gloom of the car park towards a door set in the far wall. He turns the handle, slips inside, and lets it fall shut behind him with a *boom*.

I'm alone.

I whip out Chloe's phone to call the police. But there's no reception down here. To save the person in the boot, I need to get out of this car park.

I run back to the roller door. There are no controls. It can only be opened from somewhere else in the building.

If I can't get out that way, and I can't go into the lift, my only option is to follow the driver. I creep up to the door he walked through and listen. Silence.

I try the handle. It won't turn.

It worked for him—why not for me? I can't see a key-hole, a button, a fingerprint, or retinal scanner.

A featureless square of plastic adorns the wall at about waist height. I prod it a couple of times and see no reaction.

Chloe once had a cat named Chimp, who slept in her bed and woke her by attacking her hair. A transmitter in his collar unlocked the electronic cat door as he approached, ensuring that he could come and go as he pleased.

Perhaps this plastic square is a sensor. The operative could have had an identity card in his wallet, which the sensor detected before unlocking the door for him. Whatever the explanation, I can't open it. I'm trapped down here.

An air vent is recessed into the wall beside the lift. I press my face up against the grille to see an enormous iron block, suspended just above the floor by seven steel cables. I don't know much about lifts, but I suppose the car must be at the top floor, since the counterweight is so close to the ground.

I could possibly break through the grille, but my shoulders and hips are too wide to fit through the vent. And I'm not sure what I'd do once I got in there.

An icy breeze sweeps up my back. The bomb-disposal robots stare at me with bulbous, glassy eyes. But they're not switched on. Looking, but not seeing.

I have more in common with them than I do with Becky, Graeme, and Kylie. More mineral than animal, I too am nothing more than a means to an end. A puppet for human masters. Unlike them, I have control over my own movements, but the same could be said of an automatic vacuum cleaner.

A tide of bitterness rises up my throat. I don't hate Chloe for making me—it's good that I'm here for her parents, and for Becky—but I resent the Open AI Community. It's bad enough being trapped in this position. I shouldn't also have to feel, or think, or hurt.

I sigh and take a few pictures of the helicopter. Up close, it looks much bulkier than it did in the air. The blades have retracted to half their normal length. The nose is broad and flat, like that of a giant snake. The wheels, which looked from a distance like ordinary truck tyres, are corrugated as if designed to climb sand dunes.

If I ever get out of here, I can take these pictures to the police—but I don't know how I would explain where I got them.

A wailing siren fills the air.

At first I'm relieved—and then I realize it's not a police car. The noise is coming from the upper floors. Someone must have seen the key jammed into the car boot, and realized that there was an intruder.

I scan the car park for somewhere to hide. But it's too open. There are no nooks to slip into.

My gaze settles on the open helicopter door. Would the soldiers think to look inside?

I step in. For such a big vehicle, it's surprisingly cramped— like an attic full of junk. Med kits and radios dangle from carbon-fibre hooks. The walls are spiderwebbed with nylon straps.

If I close the door, they might notice. Instead, I shrink into the shadows between the two seats up the front of the aircraft.

The cargo lift opens.

I watch through the tinted windscreen as two soldiers emerge, gripping thick-barrelled handguns. Their eyes sweep the gloom for a moment before they split up, one moving towards the far side of the car park, the other approaching the helicopter.

I stare at him, willing him to turn away. He doesn't. When he's close enough, he crouches to look under the helicopter. Then he rises and circles around towards the open door.

If I move, he'll know I'm here. But if I don't, he'll see me when he climbs on board. And I don't know if that shotgun is loaded with beanbag rounds.

I hesitate for a fraction of a second. Then I jump to my feet and pull on the door.

The soldier's yell is cut off as the door slams closed. I wrench the handle sideways to lock it, just in time. His hands scrabble at the outside of the hull, to no avail.

I pace back and forth, tugging at my wig. I've trapped myself twice over. I'm stuck in the helicopter, which is stuck in the car park. What can I do?

The other soldier runs towards the helicopter, gun raised. Looking past him, I see the roller door, wondering if Becky is still on the other side of it, wondering if I'll ever see her again—

An idea materializes in my head. It's dangerous. Crazy, maybe. But I've run out of other options.

I sit down in the pilot's chair. Graeme once told Chloe that most military vehicles could be started at the touch of a button. On the battlefield, no soldier wanted to have to fumble with keys.

The control panel has a lot of buttons and switches. I ignore all the ones which look like they control the rotor—I only need the wheels—and push a yellow button. Suddenly the car park is bright orange in the glow from the running lights. A red button activates a siren, which competes with the alarms already echoing through the car park.

The green button, half-hidden behind a plastic cap, starts the engine.

I pull on my seat belt as a roaring fills the air. The controls are nothing like those of a car. There is no steering wheel, no accelerator, no brake. Instead, there are two rubber-handled levers. As a child, Chloe had a remote-control car which worked a bit like this—one lever for the left set of wheels, another for the right. It meant that the car could rotate on the spot, without having to drive in big circles.

I throw both levers forward and the helicopter lurches out of the parking space. The two soldiers back away as the aircraft rumbles across the concrete.

The lift arrives again, this time with four more soldiers.

I adjust the levers so the helicopter swerves left. Soon it's facing the roller door.

I grab both rubber handles and push them forward with all my might.

The helicopter zooms towards the roller door, gaining speed with every second. I clench my teeth and brace myself against the chair as it rockets up the ramp.

The impact throws me forward so hard that the seat belt cuts into my shoulders. There's a deafening groan as the nose of the aircraft crumples against the roller door.

Which is still standing.

I gape at the door as the helicopter rolls backwards down the ramp. What is it made of? How could it possibly survive a ramming attack from a helicopter?

I shriek and throw my arms over my face as a hailstorm of bullets slams into the side of the aircraft. Through dozens of ragged holes in the hull, I can see one of the soldiers manning the belt-fed machine gun mounted on the utility vehicle. As I watch, he opens fire a second time and the helicopter tilts sideways as the air is filled with the sound of popping tyres and the stench of spilled petrol.

I turn back to the controls. This isn't over yet.

I hit the switch marked *activate rotor*.

The helicopter blades extend above me with a sound like swords being drawn, and then the noise is drowned out by the whining of the engine, louder than before.

Another lever is marked *altitude*. Hoping that this controls the rotor speed, I pull it right up.

The air shudders as though a thunderstorm has appeared in the car park. The wheels start to lift off the ground, and I push the altitude lever back down until they settle. Then I grab the wheel controls again and push them forward. The deflated tyres grind up the ramp.

The helicopter blades emit a piercing shriek as they slice into the roller door. Sparks fly and molten metal drips as the friction turns into volcanic heat. A slit of daylight appears across the door, but the impact has forced the chopper back down the ramp. I push it forward again. The engine roars. The helicopter blades dig into the roller door again, widening the hole.

Another shower of bullets hits the hull. I ignore them and pull the altitude lever all the way up, cranking the rotor to its maximum speed.

One of the blades snaps off and flies at the wall, where it digs into the concrete like an arrow in a tree trunk. Even without it, I can feel the wheels lifting off the ground again.

The roller door's last joint tears open and the bottom half of it collapses. The bullet-ridden wheels now won't turn at all, so I push another lever which angles the rotor forwards. The aircraft half flies, half drags itself through the gap, engine smoking, blades cutting chips of cement out of the doorway.

The helicopter is barely halfway out before I unlock the door and throw myself clear. Becky is crouched behind the skip bin, and I sprint past her, yelling 'Move move move!' before the aircraft catches fire behind me with a *WHUMPFF.*

I risk a glance back in time to see two more operatives at the opposite end of the alley, rifles slung under their arms, before my view is obscured by the enormous petals of smoke blossoming out of the helicopter's fuel tank. Becky is right behind me, hair sticking to her sweaty face.

In seconds we're turning the corner onto the main street. We need to run, but we also need to blend in. The easiest way to make that happen is to ensure that everybody else is running too.

'Fire!' I yell. 'Go! Run! Fire!'

For a second nothing happens, but then one person starts backing away, and someone else starts running, and then two people copy him, and then suddenly Becky and I are at the centre of a panicked crowd, flooding up the street away from the alleyway.

Over the yelling and heavy breathing and pounding feet, I can hear sirens on the breeze. Hera Global is about to find themselves with some explaining to do.

A few blocks up, I stop running.

'Chloe,' Becky yells, perhaps forgetting who I really am. 'Come on!'

'Hang on,' I say. 'There's a pay phone.'

'The cops are already on their way,' Becky says.

'Yeah.' I'm already moving towards the phone. 'But they don't know what to look for.'

I search my pockets for a coin, and then realize that it's probably free to call emergency services. I dial.

'Fire, Ambulance, or Police?' a voice says. Calm, but somehow impatient at the same time.

'Police,' I say, in the masculine voice of Chloe's favourite rapper. Becky stares at me. 'I just saw . . .'

'Hold, please.'

The phone rings again.

'Police. What is your location?'

'Corner of Chan Street and Benjamin Way,' I say. 'I just saw someone get shoved into the boot of a car.'

'Can you describe the victim?'

'I didn't get a good look. But the driver was about a

hundred and ninety centimetres, ninety kilos. Caucasian, brown hair. Bruises on his chin. He took the car into the alleyway behind the big glass building.'

'What's your name, sir?'

'People are running,' I say. 'There's some kind of fire. I have to go.'

I hang up.

~

It takes us a few minutes to run to the bus station and a few more to find a bus going in the right direction. Once we're on board, we start tidying our hair and clothes, trying not to look like we just walked off the set of a disaster film.

'That was really brave,' Becky murmurs. 'Going in there.'

I shrug uncomfortably.

'I wouldn't have done that. Nor would Chloe.'

'What would Chloe have done?'

Becky looks out the window. 'I don't know. She wasn't shy, exactly, but she was always afraid of inconveniencing people. No matter how much they deserved it.'

She didn't worry about inconveniencing me—not after she discovered she was being stalked.

'Maybe she had more to lose,' I say.

'Maybe.' Becky looks reluctant to compare me to my predecessor. 'So what happens now?'

'I don't know. Hopefully the police will find the remains of the helicopter, they'll rescue the guy from the boot of the car, and they'll charge Ares with everything.'

'And if they don't?'

'Then we'll give them the pictures of the driver,' I say. 'I just have to work out a plausible reason to have them.'

The bus rumbles to a halt at my stop, and I stand.

'Call me, OK?' says Becky. 'Tomorrow.'

I nod. 'Sure.' Then I tromp off the bus and start walking home.

The shadows grow along the footpath. Dead leaves crunch under my shoes.

I'm ten minutes later than I told Graeme I would be, but his car isn't in the driveway, so I'm not caught. A lucky break. I unlock the front door and walk in.

I find Kylie in the living room, re-alphabetizing the books on the shelves. 'Hey sweetie,' she says. 'You're home late.'

'You're home early,' I counter. 'How come?'

'The office closed early so the exterminators could have free rein. Which, by the way, is what the mice have had for years.'

'Where's Dad?'

'Stuck in traffic, I imagine. The radio said there was some kind of explosion in Belconnen—apparently no one was hurt, but a lot of people are gridlocked.'

'An accidental explosion?'

'No. The police think it was a botched robbery of one of the offices around there.'

Not far from the truth. 'Wow,' I say. 'So soon after the school was attacked?'

'I know. People kept calling the radio station to say that we wouldn't have these problems if we didn't let so many refugees into the country. The host was more polite to the callers than he should have been—I got mad and turned it off.'

The doorbell rings.

Kylie sighs. 'Your father must have lost his keys again. Go let him in, will you?'

I trot back to the front door. Open it.

'Hi Chloe,' Detective Anders says.

Detective Ericson is right behind her. Neither of them is smiling.

My chest implodes with panic. How can they have found me already?

'Is your mother home?' Anders asks.

'Who is it?' Kylie calls from the other room.

I say nothing. It's over.

Kylie arrives behind me, and sees the police. 'What's this about?' she demands.

'I'm afraid I have some bad news, Ms Samuels,' Anders says. 'Your husband is dead.'

THE PINBOARD

Anders' mouth keeps moving, but I no longer recognize the sounds coming out of it as words. Only fragments make it through the haze. 'Accident . . . vehicle . . . roll-over . . . dental records . . . '

It feels as though my chest is filling up with jagged shards of ice. It's like I'm going to pass out, or throw up.

My dad is dead. The man who checked under my bed for monsters when I was a little girl. Who carried me on his shoulders when we went to the supermarket, and didn't mind when I pulled his hair. Who held my doll's house still while I applied glue and glitter.

None of that was you, says a gloomy voice in my head. That was Chloe.

But I remember it. It's all so real.

'No,' Kylie whispers. 'No, no, no!' All the blood has drained from her face. She sways as though standing in a canoe.

I touch her arm, steadying her. She doesn't react.

'Perhaps we could come inside,' Detective Ericson says.

'I . . . OK,' Kylie says. But she doesn't stand aside until Anders steps into the doorway and gently bumps into her.

I follow them, forgetting to close the door. My dad is dead. My dad is dead.

The police find the living room on their own, and sit down on the couch. Kylie and I copy them, sinking into rocking chairs which creak and groan.

We all sit there for a moment without saying anything. I can hear a quiet keening from within Kylie's throat.

'I know this is hard,' Anders says finally. 'But we're going to have to ask you some questions. Is that OK?'

I swallow the bile—or whatever it is—rising up my throat. 'Do you need us to identify the body?'

The body. My father, reduced to an object.

Ericson shakes his head. 'You wouldn't be able to. He . . . '

'He's already been identified,' Anders says carefully. 'Don't worry about that. We're just trying to fill in the timeline leading up to his death. What time did he leave for work this morning?'

'Um.' Kylie's voice wobbles. Another tear tumbles down her cheek. 'About . . . about seven-thirty.'

He offered me a lift to school. I should have taken it. I wish I'd known it would be my last chance to spend any time with him.

'Did he usually leave at about that time?'

Kylie's fists tremble in her lap. 'I guess so. I don't know. I . . . '

'When would you typically expect him home?'

'I don't know,' Kylie says again. 'I get home at six-ish. He's usually here when I arrive.'

'So, by the time the vehicle was found . . . '

'Six twenty-eight,' Ericson says.

'He was already a little late,' Anders says. 'Is that right?'

'I guess so,' Kylie says. Her breaths are fast and shallow. 'What does that mean?'

'Accidents often involve drivers who are running late for something,' Anders says. 'Especially single car incidents like this one—a roll-over happens when a driver takes a corner too quickly. But we were hoping to clear up a discrepancy. He actually left work at one-fifteen today.'

'He did?'

Kylie and I look at each other. The pain in her red-rimmed eyes is unbearable. I turn back to the cops.

'Do you know where he might have been going?' Anders asks.

'I can't think of anything,' Kylie says.

'He didn't mention an appointment? Lunch with a friend, maybe?'

She shakes her head. 'I'm sorry. Maybe . . . someone at his office might know.'

'We'll have a talk with them later,' Anders says. 'What time did you leave work today?'

'About five-forty, I guess.'

'When did you get home?'

'Six-ish.'

'OK.' Anders turns to me. 'What about you, Chloe? What time did you leave school?'

'I finished at three o'clock.'

'And when did you arrive here?'

I can't lie about this in front of Kylie. 'Just a few minutes ago.' Then, because it will seem less suspicious if I volunteer the information, I say, 'I caught the bus from school

164

into Belconnen for a hot chocolate with my friend Becky, and then I caught another one home.'

'What's Becky's last name?'

'Lieu. L-I-E-U.' I remember telling Graeme the same thing.

'She goes to Scullin High with you?'

'Yes.'

Anders and Ericson look at each other. 'I think that's all we need,' Anders says.

They stand up to leave.

'Did anyone see the crash?' I ask.

Anders shakes her head. 'A passing motorist saw the overturned car afterwards.'

'Was Dad alive when the ambulance arrived?'

'The car was on fire,' Ericson says. 'But your father was still wearing his seat belt, so it looks like he was killed on impact, and the fire started afterwards. We'll have to wait for the coroner's report to be sure, of course.'

'It would have been very quick,' Anders says. 'He wouldn't have felt any pain.'

My stomach is a twisted, aching ball. When Chloe felt this sick as a little girl, she'd beg her father to make the agony stop somehow. But now he's not here to help. He'll never be here again.

How can a machine feel grief? And how can I be thinking about myself at a time like this?

'Is there someone you can call?' Anders asks.

'For what?' Kylie asks.

'To talk to.'

'Oh.'

After a pause, I say, 'Dad's sister lives in Borneo. We'll try calling her.'

Anders can see that Kylie isn't in good shape. 'Is there anybody nearby who could come over?'

Henrietta's parents live in Macgregor, less than ten minutes' drive away. 'I'll phone Michael and Sally,' I tell Kylie. 'OK?'

'OK.'

Anders and Ericson look at one another, communicating without words. I can tell that Anders is suspicious of me—this is the third time we've met in three days, and cops don't like coincidences. But she knows that this isn't the time for an interrogation.

'We'll call you when we know more,' she says finally. 'I'm sorry for your loss.'

I get up and lead the two police officers back to the front door. They trudge out and close it behind them. Silence falls. It's like being inside a sunken ship.

When I go back into the living room, Kylie is standing in front of the couch, staring at the spot where Graeme usually sits. It's like my heart is breaking. I never thought I could feel so much. I'd give anything to make it stop.

'I'm so sorry, Mum,' I say.

She wraps her arms around me and sobs into my hair. She seems so small.

I rub her shoulders until she lets me go.

'I'll call Hen's parents,' I say.

As though I might have forgotten, she says, 'The phone's in the kitchen.'

I squeeze her arm, and walk over to the phone, my feet heavy. I dial Henrietta and listen to it ring, and ring.

'Hello?' It's Henrietta's mother.

'It's Chloe,' I say.

'Oh, hi! I'll just find Henrietta for you.'

'No, wait . . .'

But she's already yelling, 'Hen! Chloe's on the line!'

I wait for Henrietta to pick up, chewing my lip. It doesn't take long.

'Hey Chloe! I was just about to call you. Pete got out of hospital a couple of hours ago, and he hasn't called me yet, but I was thinking about calling him and I wondered how long you thought I should wait. Chloe?'

It's like getting strangled by the soldier.

'Chloe? Are you still there?'

'My dad's dead,' I say and, though my eyes are stinging and my cheeks are burning, it's not until the first droplet has reached my mouth that I realize I can cry.

~

When the doorbell rings, I'm on the couch with my arms around Mum/Kylie. Neither of us has stopped weeping. I can't stop thinking about Dad/Graeme and his relationship with Chloe/me.

Human and machine are dissolving into one another. A machine couldn't hurt this much. But a human couldn't survive a decapitation, or walk unaffected through chloroflurane gas. It's like I'm standing on two platforms as they slide further and further apart.

When I answer the door, Henrietta and her parents come straight in. Sally wears a woollen scarf and knee-high boots despite the heat. She's carrying a packet of chocolate biscuits—Chloe's favourite brand.

Whenever I had a cold, Dad used to cook mini-quiches for dinner, because he knew how much I loved them. I never told him that my nose was too blocked to taste anything.

Chloe, not me. Graeme, not Dad. And now Henrietta has arranged for her dad to bring Chloe's favourite kind of biscuits, and still I won't be able to taste them.

Michael, a short, slender man in a dark polo shirt, walks over to Kylie and sweeps her into a hug, while Sally hovers awkwardly in the doorway. Henrietta sees me, and runs over, arms outstretched. Her eyes are brimming over with tears, which sets me off again. I try to blink away the hot droplets in my eyes.

Chloe's voice echoes through my skull. *The pain isn't real. The fear isn't real. These are pre-programmed responses that you don't need.*

How can fake emotions hurt so much?

'Chloe,' Henrietta says. 'I'm so sorry.'

I hug her. 'Thanks for coming.'

'I'll put the kettle on,' Sally is saying. 'Who takes milk?'

I nod, because Chloe would have.

'What happened?' Henrietta is asking me. 'Was there another car?'

'Just Dad's,' I say. 'The cops said it rolled over on a corner. He wouldn't—they said he felt no pain.'

Henrietta sniffles. 'Let me get you some tissues,' I say. I head for Chloe's room, and Henrietta follows me.

'Where were you?' she asks. 'When it happened?'

I pull a handful of tissues out of a box on Chloe's bedside table and hand them over. 'I was on my way home from school,' I say. 'And just after I got here, the police came, and then . . . and now I don't know what to do.'

She squeezes my hand. 'Don't worry, OK? I'm here for you.'

'Thanks, Hen.'

There's a knock at the door. Michael comes in with two mugs of tea. 'Are you OK?' he asks me.

I nod. 'Don't worry about me.'

Henrietta takes her tea and sips it. 'Thanks, Dad.'

Her eyes are starting to look wet again. Perhaps she's wondering what she'd do without him.

'Is there anything else I can get you?' he asks me. 'Fancy a biscuit?'

'Maybe later,' I say. 'Thanks.'

He leaves the room, reluctantly.

'Your dad was the world's safest driver,' Henrietta says. 'How could this have happened?'

'I don't know.' Because he was stressed, perhaps. The shock is fading now, and I'm starting to look at this in the context of what's happened over the last few days. Graeme left work early today, and apparently didn't tell anyone why. That could mean he was going to meet with Nadine.

After that, he drove halfway home before veering off the road and rolling his car. There has to be a reason for that. It can't just be bad luck.

What if someone was chasing him? Someone from Ares?

My plastic guts lurch in my belly. I'd give anything to bring him back.

Henrietta hugs me again. 'I know,' she says, although I've said nothing aloud. 'I know.'

I cry in her arms for a moment. She strokes my shuddering back. Henrietta has always been there for me—for Chloe—no matter what. And what have I given her in return? Lies. About what I am, about what I did this afternoon, about what I suspect happened to Graeme.

We're supposed to be best friends, but even in life Chloe wasn't as supportive as she should have been. Henrietta gave much more to the relationship than she did.

'Last year,' I say. 'When you weren't well.'

'Shh.'

On camping trips, Graeme used to tell Chloe ghost stories. She loved the chills that ran down her spine as she listened. The ghosts always appeared because in life they'd left something unsaid or undone.

Maybe if Chloe had lived, she would have made up for the things she did or didn't do. But it's too late for her. It has to be me.

'I'm sorry I wasn't there for you,' I say. 'I should have listened. I should have watched more closely. I . . . '

'Shut up.' Henrietta squeezes me tighter. 'You were— you are—the best friend I could ever wish for.'

When she releases me, I dab at my eyes with tissues. By the time they're dry, I can feel a little of Chloe's guilt has left my chest.

You're going to look after Mum while I'm gone.

'We should check on my Mum,' I say.

'OK,' Henrietta says.

We stand up, and go to join the others in the living room.

Kylie clings to her teacup, but doesn't drink. A trickle of scalding tea tips over the side onto her hand. She doesn't react. I've lost my father and my mother in the same day.

'I can make some calls,' Sally is saying. 'About the funeral, and the will. Who's your lawyer?'

'I'm not sure. Graeme takes care of . . . took care of . . . ' Kylie trails off.

Sally and Michael exchange glances. 'It's OK, sweetie,'

170

Sally says. 'We'll figure it out.'

I rest my hand on top of Kylie's head and stroke her hair, like she did when Chloe was a little girl and couldn't sleep. But my silicon skin sticks to her hair, making it hard to avoid creating knots.

'I'd better call Dad's sister,' I say.

Kylie says, 'I can . . .' and then she stops, perhaps realizing that she can't.

I pick up the phone and head back to my room. Henrietta says, 'Want me to come with you?'

'It's OK,' I say. 'It's better if I do this by myself. I'll be right back.'

~

I can't sleep.

After hours of hugging and weeping, Henrietta's family has gone home. I'm in bed, feeling the mattress sink further than it should.

Graeme's sister isn't coming back for the funeral. Michael and Sally were surprised to hear that. Kylie and I weren't.

'It costs almost five hundred dollars to get home from Borneo,' Chloe's aunt told me. 'And another five hundred to get back. You know how many clean-water facilities we could build with that money? How many lives we could save?'

It's hard to argue with a humanitarian. It was only as she was saying those words that I remembered something that made me shiver: as a little girl, Chloe had suspected her aunt might be a robot.

I haven't been able to sleep on any previous night either, but this time it hurts more. This time I have to listen to the voice in my head that says Chloe's dead and Graeme's dead and it's all my fault, somehow. As I walked past Kylie's room earlier I saw her standing beside her bed, staring at it as though she already couldn't remember which side of it was hers. The sight triggered another flood of tears.

In my two-day life, I had lied to Graeme, spied on him, and stolen his car. I didn't do a single good thing for him, and now I'll never get the chance.

I glare at the ceiling, willing it to collapse and bludgeon me unconscious. I need to sleep. Why didn't Chloe or the Open AI Community programme a sleep function into my code?

The clock reads 22:16:40. Eight more hours of this, at least.

I pick up my mobile phone and call Becky. It takes a few rings before she answers.

'Hello?' It sounds like she's just woken up.

'It's me,' I say, somewhat nervously.

'I know. Are you OK?'

'Not really,' I say. 'I can't sleep. Too much thinking.'

'Thinking? That's never a good idea. Want me to come over?'

'I'll come to you,' I say. 'What's your address?'

She tells me where she lives and how to get past the back fence to her bedroom window. I thank her, tell her I'll be there soon, and hang up.

Sneaking out of the house brings back guilty memories of my first night here. If I had stayed, would Chloe still be alive?

Stop thinking, I tell myself. Thinking is a bad idea.

I creep out the front door and onto the street, where I start jogging towards Becky's house. Chloe uploaded some maps of the city to my head, so I know which way to go. I even know how exactly how many kilometres it is and how long it will take me—fifty minutes at this speed.

My slapping footsteps bounce back off the dark houses, making it sound like someone's chasing me. I have to keep turning my head to check that they're not.

Thoughts of Becky ease the tension. I haven't known her long, but already she feels like the only safe part of my world.

A stray cat sees me, glares, and slinks away into a drain.

Becky's house is small, probably three cosy bedrooms and one bathroom, but pretty, with big windows overlooking a garden of native plants.

I trot through the car port, reach over the gate for the latch, and sneak into the back yard. A big umbrella looms over some spindly chairs and a small table, which supports a pair of forgotten coffee mugs. A skate ramp, two metres high in a quarter-pipe shape, sits on the dirt by the fence.

Becky's window is the last one along. I reach up and tap the glass.

She rolls up the window and leans out. A dressing gown is wrapped around her shoulders. 'Hey Chloe,' she says.

'I'm not Chloe,' I remind her.

'Do you have another name I should know about?'

'No.'

'Then I'm going to call you Chloe,' she says.

'Nice skate ramp.'

'It was my brother's. I can't skate, but it felt wrong to throw it away. Come on in.'

She braces her foot against the windowsill and holds out both hands. I grab them, and she helps me walk up the wall—two steps and I'm up and over, landing on the soft carpet of her room.

She slides the window closed. 'You're heavier than she was.'

'Are you saying I'm fat?'

She laughs and switches on her bedside lamp. Becky's bedroom isn't very teenage—no posters, no speakers, no box of outgrown toys. The only wall that isn't covered by bookshelves seems to have been drawn on. An intricate sketch of a waterfall in a forest covers it from ceiling to floor. There's a blank spot in the bottom right-hand corner.

'So,' she says. 'You've been thinking.'

I take a deep breath. 'My dad—I mean, Chloe's dad—died this afternoon.'

Becky's mouth falls open. 'Oh my God,' she says. 'I'm so sorry! What happened?'

She hugs me. The last time we were this close, we were in the girls' bathroom and I was covering her mouth so she couldn't scream. Such intimate contact may not seem weird to her—she and Chloe were in love, after all. But it feels very strange to me.

'It was a car accident,' I say. 'I told the police I was with you when it happened. At the café. They might call you.'

'Don't worry about that,' she says. 'I'll tell them the same thing.' She lets go of me. 'How's your mum?'

'Not good. She didn't stop crying all night.'

'And what about you? How are you coping?'

I say nothing. *Machines don't have rights. If anyone finds out what you are, they'll take you apart to see how you work.*

Chloe was probably right about a lot of people. But she misjudged Becky. Knowing what I am hasn't stopped her from considering my feelings. In fact, when she thought I was human, she spent her time glaring across the classroom at me. She treats me much better now.

'I'm OK,' I say. I'm not, but I don't know how to say so. 'Did you draw that?'

She looks over at the wall. 'You don't remember?'

I shake my head.

'The wall is coated with plastic, like a whiteboard. Drawing on it helps clear my head. Every time I fill up the space, I take a photo of it and then wipe it all off and start a new sketch.' Her gaze traces the lines of the water. 'Chloe helped me draw this one.'

Why did she leave that out of my memories? 'When was that?'

Becky sits on the bed. 'On the day before Pete's party, Mr Fresner partnered us up for a computing exercise. It was awful. I'd had a crush on Chloe for months, but I'd never dared to speak to her, and now we were doing this coding thing together, and it couldn't have been more obvious that I had no idea what I was doing. But she was really nice about it. She offered to come over after school and show me some things. I wanted to believe she was flirting with me, but it felt like wishful thinking.' She blushes. 'Sorry. You probably don't want to hear this.'

I sit next to her. 'No, I want to know. What happened when she came over?'

'She brought her laptop, and helped me out with some of the things I'd struggled with. Then we just sat, right here, and chatted about other stuff. For hours. She told me about her mum and dad, and Henrietta, and her clarinet—everything. And I told her about my brother, and his skateboarding, and my basketball team, and the wall.' She

175

points to a part that seems rougher than the rest. 'That part was hers. I don't think I'll ever wipe it off.'

We stare at the picture for a moment.

'Did she . . . '

'Make a move on me?' Becky smiles sadly. 'No. The whole time she was here, my heart was thumping—I wanted to touch her, but I was so scared that she would freak out, so I didn't do anything. Eventually she left, and I lay awake all night wondering what I should have done.'

'And the next day, you were both at Pete's party.'

'Right. I couldn't bear the thought of going home without knowing, and trying to make it through another night. So I asked her to come with me to the porch, and I told myself to be brave, and I opened my mouth to confess . . . and she kissed me.'

This doesn't sound at all like the Chloe I met. She was cold. Ruthless.

But she wasn't always that way. As a Year Two student, Chloe informed the kid who sat next to her that he was now her boyfriend. When asked what a boyfriend did, Chloe said he would be required to hold her hand. He nodded thoughtfully, and said, 'I can do that.'

I remember a tingling sensation in her belly as the boy's fingers were intertwined with hers at recess. For some reason, I have that feeling now.

'When was the next time you saw her?' I ask.

The smile fades from Becky's lips. 'I expected her to call over the weekend, but she didn't. I didn't call her, either. I didn't want to seem desperate. And then she didn't show up for school on Monday. When I asked her form tutor he said someone had called to confirm she was at a girls' development camp. And when she came back, she completely ignored me. It was like she wanted to forget the whole thing.'

I put my arm around her. 'I'm sorry.'

'It's not your fault. I just wish I had the chance to say goodbye.'

We sit in silence for a while.

'I never said goodbye to Graeme, either,' I say. 'I only knew him for two days, and that whole time I never once told him the truth.'

'You couldn't. It would have destroyed both of you.'

'But now he's dead anyway.' My lip trembles. 'He died believing I was his daughter.'

Becky rubs my back. 'When I was a little girl,' she says, 'my brother told me this theory he had. He said that our bodies were like pinboards, and our memories were like photographs. Basically, he thought that the only function of our bodies was to carry our memories around.'

'Interesting idea.'

'He was an interesting guy,' she says. 'He died almost ten months ago. He had muscular dystrophy.'

I take her hand. 'I'm sorry.' In less than a year, Becky has had to grieve for both her girlfriend and her sibling.

'Me too. The last time I spoke to him, he was in a lot of pain and on a lot of drugs, but he did manage to say something. He said, "The pinboard is all worn out. But you can keep the photos."'

'Because you'd still have your memories of him?'

'Yeah,' she says. 'I think that's what he meant.'

'Why are you telling me this?'

'Because if all that's left of Graeme is memories, and you have all Chloe's memories of him, then he was right about you. In every way that matters, you *are* his daughter.'

'I'm worried that I'll forget him,' I say. 'Not everything about him, but little pieces, one at a time, until there's nothing special left.'

'Don't your memories last for ever?'

'No. The people who designed my brain wanted it to be realistic, so they programmed them to fade.'

'That's terrible,' she says.

'I know.'

'Maybe we can hack it.'

'Hack what?' I ask. 'My brain?'

'Sure. Your code is the problem, so we change the code.'

It hadn't occurred to me to try that. 'Do you know how to do that?'

She shrugs. 'I don't know how it's set up, obviously. But I can take a look. If it's just one sub-routine, I can try to disable it. I mean, if you want me to.'

The idea of changing my programming is seductive. It feels like my first chance to decide who I'm going to be, instead of following someone else's script. Literally.

'OK,' I say. 'Let's do it.'

There's a pause.

Becky says, 'How do I . . . is there a USB port in your head, or anything?'

I laugh nervously. 'I don't know.'

She touches my hair, parting it, nails gently raking across my scalp. A tingle zips down my spine.

'There's nothing there,' she says.

'I didn't see any cables when Chloe first woke me up,' I say.

'What about a router? Maybe you have Wi-Fi.'

'Maybe. How could I tell?'

'Just a sec.' Becky pulls a netbook off her bookshelves and switches it on.

After a few seconds of fiddling, she says, 'Yeah, here you are.' She turns the reader around to show me a list of 'devices'. One of them is called 'Chloe'.

Seeing my brain on a list of computers makes me feel dizzy. 'Can you access it?'

She tries. 'Nope. Password protected.'

I tell her Chloe's email password. 'Try that.'

She taps the screen a few times, and blinks. 'I'm in.'

I close my eyes, wondering if I'll be able to feel her intrusion. But there's nothing.

'Can you see the code?'

She looks nervous. 'There's a lot of files, including a config document for memory.'

What have I got to lose? 'Open it,' I say.

'I can't,' she says, after a pause. 'Not while your systems are running.'

'Then switch me off,' I say. 'I could use some sleep.'

~

When I wake up, the clock resting against the books on one of Becky's shelves tells me that almost an hour has passed. Longer than I expected.

'How do you feel?' she asks. She's sitting cross-legged on her bed, the netbook closed beside her.

'Smart,' I say. 'No, that's not quite right. Knowledgeable.'

'You still remember who you are, and everything? You remember me?'

I nod. 'And more. What did you do to me?'

'I removed the limitations on your memory and processing speed,' she says. 'Then I gave you some new memories to test the modifications.'

'Like what?'

'I found the folder in your system where books are stored. Chloe had told me about some authors that she'd always wanted to read, but never found the time. So I uploaded their complete bibliographies. You've read almost two hundred more books now than you had before.'

I search the inside of my own head. It's true. I can name – and summarize—all the novels and short stories by Mary Shelley, Phillip K. Dick, and many other writers.

'She also told me she wanted to travel,' Becky continues. 'She wanted to see Malaysia, Russia, and Uganda. Now she never will, but I thought maybe if I gave you pictures and maps and histories of those countries, that would be the next best thing. I gave you some programming knowledge, too—in case we can find Ares' backup servers.'

Images flash up in my head as she names the countries. I know the faces on the bank notes, the names of the politicians and the locations of the landmarks.

Becky's hair has fallen across her cheek. I want to tuck it behind her ear. In fact, I want more than that. She's so clever, so kind. I want to lean in and kiss her beautiful mouth. The longing is so strong it hurts.

And yet I'm frozen in place. I have no hormones to pump through my brain. No blood to colour my cheeks. No heart to beat faster at the sight of Becky. These sensations are fake. Does that mean my feelings are, too? Does it matter?

Part of me wonders if she programmed me to love her while I was unconscious. But the rest of me knows that I've wanted her since we met, even if I've only just admitted it to myself.

The authenticity of my emotions is only half the equation. How would Becky feel about dating Chloe's ghost?

'I know you're not her,' Becky says, as if she could hear my thoughts. Her voice wobbles. 'I do know that. But I think she would have liked you to . . . to become the woman that she always wanted to be.'

Her tears choke off the last word. The almost-kiss forgotten, I wrap her up in a hug. Her body jerks as she pulls in sob after shuddering sob.

'It's OK,' I say, rubbing my palm against her back. I'm not sure if she hears me. 'Chloe wouldn't have wanted you to be sad.'

She keeps crying. I can feel my shoulder getting wet. 'I miss her so much,' she gasps.

'I know. But I'm going to take care of you. We're going to take care of each other. OK?'

'OK,' she says miserably. 'OK.'

I spend the night at Becky's place, lying beside her on top of the sheets, stroking her hair until she falls asleep. My fingers stick to the strands, so I use a pencil instead.

To pass the time, I re-read some of the books installed in my head, and brush up on my Russian history. The amount of knowledge that has been crammed into my brain is spectacular. I could give presentations on it.

If only Chloe's story were so clear. I don't know why Ares followed her rather than Graeme, or why her school was their target, or why her father drove his car off the road. And I have no idea how to find any of it out.

After chasing my thoughts around in circles for a while, I

realize that if I don't leave soon I won't make it home before Kylie wakes up. I don't want to rouse Becky, so I shift away from her—slowly, gently—before climbing out of bed and exiting through the window.

I'm halfway home when I remember the thumping from the boot of the soldier's car. The muffled yelling.

Was that Graeme's voice?

THE NET, CAST

'Thanks for calling Ares Security.'

'Is this Nadine?' I ask. I keep my voice low. It's ten o'clock, but Kylie is still asleep in the next room.

'Yes,' she says. 'Sorry, who is this?'

'A friend of Graeme's.'

There's a pause.

'How did you get this number?' she whispers.

'I know a lot more than just the number,' I say. 'But I have questions. You're going to give me the answers—unless you want your bosses to find out what you've been doing.'

'Hold on,' she says. 'Don't do anything rash. We should meet. This afternoon.'

She hasn't hung up on me, so she must be talking on a secure phone. Or she thinks, she is, at least.

'Three o'clock,' I say. 'At the bookshop in the north-east corner of the Belconnen shopping centre. It's on the top floor. Come alone.'

'That's too public,' she says. 'If they see me . . .'

'Then I suggest you use a disguise.'

'How will I know you?'

She would have seen pictures of Chloe on the walls of Graeme's house. But I don't want her to know who I am until I get there.

'I'll know *you*,' I say. 'Bring a pencil. Tuck it behind your ear.'

I hang up before she has the chance to argue.

Kylie appears in the doorway. Her pyjamas are crinkled and her hair is scuffed up on one side and the skin around her eyes is bruised with exhaustion. She hasn't slept at all.

'Who was that?' she asks.

'Henrietta. Just checking that we're OK.'

Kylie nods, and squints out of the living room window.

'Can I make you some tea?' I ask.

'No. I have to go out.'

'Where to?'

'I need to arrange the funeral and talk to our lawyer,' she says. 'And there are some insurance things to deal with. I could only get two weeks off work, so I'd like to get it all out of the way.'

Graeme was the only member of our family with a decent salary. Kylie probably makes enough for us both to live off, but not to the standard we're used to. A car. A nice house, near the school and close to our friends. Food that doesn't come out of a can, or the freezer.

'You shouldn't have to go back to work so soon,' I say. 'I can get a job. At weekends, and at night.'

'No,' Kylie replies. 'With Graeme gone, I'll need you at home.'

'But we might need the extra money.'

'Your father was well covered,' Kylie says. 'We'll be OK.'

We can't live off life insurance for ever, but I don't say so. She has enough on her mind. I'll bring it up again in a few days, though. I'm strong, knowledgeable, and I don't need to eat or sleep. With the right job, I could earn more than enough to keep her above the poverty line.

Until I get found out. Then she'll have nobody.

~

The floor squeaks under my shoes as I walk past the clothes shops which thump like nightclubs, the kiosks selling cable TV subscriptions, the beauty shops adorned with bath salts and scented candles. A girl glares at an ATM with the intensity of a safe-cracker. A toddler runs past me, screaming, while his father calls his name half-heartedly.

The bookshop is up ahead, towers of bestsellers looming behind the windows. Nadine is scheduled to arrive in ten minutes; I want to see her go in before I do.

The plump couches are conspicuously close to the entrance. Instead, I stand on the opposite side of the corridor, pretending to talk on the phone. 'Uh-huh,' I say. 'Well, what did you tell him? Really?'

She arrives just as I'm running out of things to say. A woman with prematurely greying hair and hooded eyes behind flimsy-looking glasses. I don't realize it's Nadine until she's already inside the bookshop, tucking a pencil behind her ear with one hand as she touches the spines of celebrity biographies with the other.

No one seems to be following her. A few people peer through the windows of the bookshop, but they don't go in. The other browsers pass her with no apparent interest.

I watch for a minute or two before approaching the shop, keeping my head bowed even though I'm wearing a beanie and tinted sunglasses. If Ares later works out that Nadine was here and steals the footage from the security cameras, I don't want them to get a good look at me.

The smells of warm paper and carpet cleaner meet me as I walk in. Once I'm out of range of the cameras in the entrance, I amble towards the biography section, occasionally stopping to pick up a book and pretend to read a blurb.

'Can I help you find anything?' asks a cheerful staff member from behind me. The sudden noise makes me jump.

I glance back at her and smile. 'Not just yet, thanks.'

'OK. Let me know.'

Her plait dangles around her hips as she walks away.

Nadine glances over at me as I sidle up beside her. Apparently not recognizing me, she turns back to the shelves.

'Hi,' I say.

She looks at me again, taking in my clothes and my age. 'Are you here for me?' she says, uncertainly.

I've only heard her speak on the phone. She sounds different in person. Her voice is lighter. More feminine.

Even if she hasn't seen the pictures of Chloe at the house, she knows Graeme had a teenage daughter, and that I describe myself as 'a friend of his'. It's surprising that she hasn't worked out who I am . . .

Unless this isn't the real Nadine.

A chill runs through my titanium tendons. If Ares intercepted my phone call, they could have sent someone else in Nadine's place. This could be one of their soldiers.

'No, sorry,' I say, trying to look puzzled. 'Excuse me.'

I squeeze past her to the shelves on the other side of the aisle, pretending that I only said 'hi' to be polite. I select a book, examine the cover, and put it back.

'It's you, isn't it?' the woman says. 'Graeme's friend.'

I shake my head. 'I don't know any Graeme. You must have me mixed up with somebody else. See you.'

I shuffle across into the next aisle and put my sunglasses back on. Between the shelves, I can see her moving after me.

Not too fast, not too slow, I work my way out of the bookshop. 'Have a good day,' says the girl with the long plait as I step out the door. She says it too quietly and from too far away to be talking to me. The woman who isn't Nadine must be following me out.

I turn left, hoping to lose her in the bustling crowd. As I approach the giant spiral staircase, a tall man with a grey suit and a clenched jaw steps out of a phone shop and starts moving towards me.

Pretending not to notice him, I slip into the crowd and trot down the staircase. My skin remains smooth, but I can feel goosebumps rising all over my body.

I pass the first-floor exit and keep descending towards the ground. But two more Ares agents, stern and muscular, are striding towards the bottom of the staircase. It's like being a fox, watching the hounds draw closer from all sides.

I whirl around and start climbing back up to the first floor. The woman who was immediately behind me yells 'Hey, watch it!' and I mutter 'Sorry,' as I race up the stairs.

I reach the first-floor exit before the tall man does, and sprint away from the staircase towards the car park. I can't pretend that I don't know I'm being chased any more. Two pairs of shoes clop against the tiles behind me as the tall man and 'Nadine' reach this floor. Then two more pairs join them, as the other agents arrive.

The automatic door slows me down. I wave my hands frantically in front of the sensor and squeeze through the growing gap into cold daylight.

I got here by bus, so no getaway car is waiting for me but, if I can get down to the ground floor, I can flee on foot. I dash across the car park towards the ramp.

Just as I approach the ramp, a black van lurches up it and skids to a halt in front of me. The driver, a burly rhinoceros of a man, jumps out and starts running in my direction. So does his passenger.

With six people hurtling towards me from two sides, I whirl around and dash towards the edge of the car park. Maybe it will be close enough to the ground that I can jump down.

I collide with the concrete barrier and peer down at the lethal drop. The impact will split my plastic skin and break my titanium skeleton, ensuring that I can never again pass for human.

But that's probably better than whatever Ares Security plans to do to me. I climb onto the barrier and prepare to jump . . .

A crackling sound tears through the air. My skin ripples as though ants have tunnelled beneath it. The world flashes bright and dark and bright again as the chip in my head fights to process the visual data. Pixel errors swarm across the world in front of me. I try to hurl myself over the edge, but all my joints have locked together and I fall backwards instead, hitting the concrete head first. I can't move. I can't think. As far as the drop was, I'm now falling so much further, into a hole so black and cold that I'll never find my way out.

~

I wake in the back of a van, shivering and blinking as though my eyelids are trying to signal somebody with Morse code.

It takes a moment to guess what has happened—the zapping sound was a Taser. I've been electrocuted, my brain has done a hard reboot, and now I don't know where I am.

'That's correct, Mr Christiansen,' the driver is saying. A headset is clipped around his ear. 'The replica was Nadine Yumika's contact.'

Christiansen's voice is tinny in the headset speaker. 'How is that possible? The chip went missing long before the replica existed.'

'You could ask Nadine, sir.'

'No. It's too late for that.'

If he's talking to Warren Christiansen, the CEO and owner of Ares Security, then I'm not being held prisoner by a rogue unit. My captor has the full might of the company behind him. Since he's using his boss's name in front of me, he probably doesn't intend to let me live. It sounds like Nadine is already dead.

Fighting to control my twitching eyelids, I stare at the massive trees and power lines visible through the windscreen. The van isn't moving, but we're not at the shopping centre any more.

'Graeme Zimetski didn't know where the QMP was,' Christiansen says. 'If the replica doesn't either, we'll have to pick up his wife.'

Kylie. No! I lunge towards the back door of the van, but something stops me halfway. My wrists are fastened to the wall by thick rope. My feet are bound to the floor.

The driver looks over at me. There's a fat bruise under his jaw. It's one of the soldiers from Scullin High. The one who drove the car with someone in the boot.

'It's back on,' he says, and it takes me a moment to realize he's referring to me. 'I'll call you when I'm done.'

He pushes a button on his headset, unbuckles his seat belt, and climbs into the back with me.

'You murdered Graeme Zimetski,' I say.

He doesn't deny it. 'I could crack your skull open and take out your hard drive,' he says. 'Soon I'd know everything you do. But it would be easier for both of us if you just told me.'

I already know what the question is going to be. But I don't know the answer.

'Where is the quantum mechanical processor?' he says.

I say nothing. If he realizes I don't know, then he'll go after Kylie.

He belts me across the face, hard. The backs of his knuckles leave a stinging dent in my silicone cheek.

'You feel pain, don't you?' he says. 'I could do things to you that would kill a human being. But you would stay conscious and feel every moment of it. Where is the quantum mechanical processor?' I don't reply.

He hits me again, once in the face, once in the chest. I cry out, and tell myself the agony is just a simulation, but I can't make myself believe it. My synthetic nerve endings are screaming.

I'm going to die here. No one will ever know what happened to me. I'll never see Becky again.

'We know you have it!' he roars. A thread of spit flails between his lips. 'The tracking beacon sends out a pulse every forty-eight hours. We followed it to Scullin High School, but you must have got there first. Now it's underground again. Where did you hide it?'

The QMP can't be tracked underground. Now I know why Graeme hid it in the basement.

'Please, I . . .'

He pulls his fist back, like a wrecking ball ready to be swung.

'I'll tell you!' I say. 'Please, just don't hit me any more.'

'Where?'

I rack my brain for a plausible spot. Somewhere I might have hidden the QMP if I had it. Somewhere underground. Somewhere he'll have to untie me, and I can escape.

'I buried it,' I say. 'In a construction site near the motorway.'

He hauls me to my feet so as I can see out of the windscreen. The chains twist my arms behind my back. Then he climbs back into the driver's seat.

'Take me there,' he says.

~

My mind races as the van pulls up outside the half-built hotel. How long can I convince him that I'm cooperating? Will it be long enough for me to find a way to escape?

'There's security,' he says, looking out the window. 'Two guys, at least.'

'We'll have to come back at night,' I tell him.

He snorts. 'Nice try.' He opens the glovebox and pulls out a large, square pistol. The safety catch clicks off.

Fear swallows my lungs. 'You can't kill them!' I say. 'They have nothing to do with this!'

'They're in my way,' he says.

'We can sneak past. There's a fence, around the back, we can climb over it . . .'

'No.' He unlocks the cuffs around my wrists and feet. 'We're going to walk right in at the front gate. Whatever I say, you're going to back me up. If you try to warn the guards in any way, I'm going to kill them both, and then I'm going to use a power sander to grind off your hands. Understood?'

I nod. It's my fault that he's here. I can't let the security guards die.

'Good,' he says, and slips the gun into his jacket pocket before opening the back of the van. We climb out into the daylight.

Ivan, the middle-aged security guard, is standing in his booth. He looks over at us as we approach. I will him not to recognize me from my break-in on Wednesday night.

'Excuse me,' he says, stepping out of the door of the booth. 'This is a restricted area.'

'So I've been told,' says the soldier. 'My name is Aaron Thomas, and I'm a federal agent. I have a warrant to search these premises.'

He flashes a badge, and then pulls a neatly folded A4 sheet of paper from his pocket and hands it to the guard. It can't have the address of the construction site on it, since the soldier didn't know where we would be going, but Ivan doesn't seem to notice the inconsistency.

'What's this about?' he says.

'I'm afraid that's classified, sir,' says 'Aaron Thomas'.

He's very convincing. I suspect this isn't the first time he's impersonated a cop.

'Who's she?' Ivan says, looking me up and down.

'A material witness,' Thomas says. 'Open the gate, please.'

'I'll have to call the owner.'

'I wouldn't do that. Not unless you want to go to court. The Official Secrets Act prohibits off-site communication while the warrant is being executed.'

He must think Ivan isn't convinced. I can see the outline of the gun moving in his pocket, lining up with Ivan's guts.

'It won't take long,' I say. 'The sooner we're done, the sooner you can call your boss.'

Ivan looks us both up and down.

'Ten minutes,' I tell him. 'Tops.'

'OK,' he says finally, and walks over to the switch that controls the gate.

As it squeaks and rattles, Thomas walks through the gap. I follow him. When he notices that Ivan is right behind us, he stops.

'Whoa,' he says. 'Where do you think you're going?'

'You can't leave my sight,' Ivan says.

'Yes we can,' Thomas says. 'This is a matter of national security. You can't observe the search.'

'If I leave you alone, I could lose my job.'

'If you don't, you could go to prison for obstruction of justice.' The soldier steps towards Ivan, looming over him. 'It's your choice. Either you go back to your booth, or I'll be forced to arrest you.'

It only takes a few seconds for Ivan to back down. 'Ten minutes,' he says.

'Ten minutes.' Thomas turns and walks away. I follow him.

'So far, so good,' he says, once we're out of earshot. 'You might just make it through this.'

He's lying. He's already killed Graeme. He has no reason to treat me differently.

'Which way?'

I point, and we start walking towards Chloe's grave.

'Down there?' the soldier says when we reach the pit.

'Yes,' I say.

'This looks like a car park,' he says. 'The QMP could have ended up covered in concrete.'

'That was the idea.'

'Why? How would you get it back?'

'It wasn't about having it,' I say. 'It was about Ares *not* having it.'

He gives me a look halfway between suspicion and respect. Maybe he's seeing me as a threat for the first time.

An escape plan is forming in my mind.

'Someone in defence got to you,' he guesses. 'They're trying to terminate the deal.'

'Do you want the QMP or not?'

I clamber down the ladder into the pit, and he follows. I lead him to the place where the real Chloe Zimetski is buried.

'You got anything to dig with?' I ask.

He nods, and points the gun at me. 'You.'

I sigh, drop to my knees, and start shifting the dirt aside with my palms.

'You're sure this is the right spot?' he says.

'Yes.'

'How deep?'

'Not very.'

He waits until he can see a shape forming under the dirt, and then he says, 'Stand up.'

I hesitate. 'I haven't found it yet.'

He smirks. 'You think you're clever. You've got some kind of weapon buried under there with it. Stand up, and take four big steps back.'

I do, slowly.

He crouches, and starts pulling away the dirt. His eyes are down, but his head is up, so as he can watch me in his peripheral vision. The pink tip of Chloe's nose is visible.

With one sweep of Thomas's hand, more of her face is revealed.

I expected a moment of surprise. He's looking for a computer chip, and found a dead body instead. But what I get is better. He's more than surprised—he's horrified. Confused.

I scream.

The noise slices through the air like a howling jet engine. It can't be as loud as a real weaponized noise cannon, but the volume coming out of my throat is a hundred times that of the video the cops showed me. My cheeks bulge and my teeth vibrate with the force of it. I can almost feel my battery draining.

The effect on Thomas is immediate. He stumbles backwards, face contorted, hands pressed over his ears. I charge, still screaming, and hit him with a flying tackle. He slams against the ground and all the air whooshes out of him as I tear the pistol from his hand and press the barrel against his throat.

'Who *are* you?' he gasps.

I ignore the question. 'Did you really think that Ares was Hera Global's only little project?' I hiss. 'Did you think we would ignore you overstepping your boundaries so flagrantly?'

His eyes widen. 'What?'

'Shut up.' I hit him in the side of the head with the grip of the gun, and he grunts. The crunch of metal on bone makes me feel ill.

I can get rid of this one soldier, but more will come. They know who I am. They know *what* I am. Ares could destroy me—but not if I destroy them first.

I need proof. Something to show to Anders. Becky suggested hacking into their servers to get their email records.

'Where are Ares' backup servers?' I ask.

Thomas says nothing.

I push the barrel of the gun into the flesh beneath his jaw. 'I'm not going to ask again.'

'We don't have any,' Thomas says. 'It would be a security risk.'

Having committed so many crimes, that's probably true. I can't prove that they're behind the attack on the school, or Graeme's murder . . .

Unless I break into their headquarters. And not just the car park this time.

'Surrender your pass key, soldier,' I say.

He hesitates a minute too long. I hit him with the gun again. 'Hand it over!'

Thomas digs around in his pocket and produces a card. It looks like the key to a hotel room, except that it's blank on both sides. I snatch it out of his hand.

'Where is the server room at Ares HQ?'

'Don't you know?'

'Yes,' I lie. 'But I want to know where you've been *told* it is.'

'Top floor,' he says.

'I need your phone,' I say. 'Your car keys, too.'

He struggles to free the items from his pocket. I take them, rise to my feet and point the gun at him.

'Get on your knees,' I say. 'Facing away from me. Interlace your fingers behind your head.'

Fear appears in his gaze. 'Wait.'

'Do it.'

He does so, slowly. 'Please,' he says. 'I have a family.'

'So did Graeme Zimetski. Did you think about that?'

'I'm sorry. I was following orders.'

My sadness is now overwhelmed by fury. I don't think my cheeks are capable of blushing, but my whole face feels hot with rage. Thomas is right. It's not just him I want to hurt. It's Warren Christiansen. He gave the orders to stalk Chloe, to kill Graeme, to torture me—and he doesn't regret it. Yet.

I press the muzzle to the back of Thomas's head and say nothing for a few seconds, letting him think he's going to die. Then I say, 'You're going to bury her again. Exactly like she was. Then you're going to leave town and never come back. Unless you do exactly as I say . . .'

I lean in, whispering in his ear. ' . . . it'll be your face I'm wearing next time.'

He falls onto his hands and knees, trembling. I tell myself that he doesn't deserve my sympathy.

I take one last look at Chloe's face before I leave. I had half expected her to be a husk by now, flesh nibbled away by ants and worms, but her skin is still filled with lifelike colour. The only damage I can see is the bullet hole in her temple, hideous in the sunshine. Beneath it . . .

My flesh turns to ice. Through the hole, I can see the gleam of a titanium skull.

UNEARTHED

'Becky,' I say. 'The real Chloe was a machine too.'

'*What?*' Her voice crackles in the soldier's earpiece. 'That doesn't make any sense!'

'I dug up her body. It's definitely mechanical.'

I'm in the soldier's van, hurtling towards Ares headquarters. Before I left the pit, I swept some dirt over Chloe so Thomas wouldn't see what I saw—the wires, the speaker, the frayed edges of the rubber. I don't know what he would think was going on if he knew. I don't even know what *I* think is going on.

But I know this. In the eyes of the law, Chloe's murder wouldn't be a murder. It was just a computer getting broken by a stray bullet.

I passed Ivan on my way out. 'Give my colleague a couple more minutes,' I told him. 'He's nearly done.' Hopefully he'll leave Thomas alone long enough for him to bury the body again. But if he doesn't, then what? It's not actually a body. When I thought I was carefully disposing of evidence, all I was really doing was littering.

'But she was real,' Becky is saying. 'I felt her body heat, and her breathing, and her pulse. At Pete's birthday party.'

I feel a stab of jealousy. I don't have any of those things, and Becky must have noticed.

'She must have been replaced after that,' I say.

Graeme's voice echoes through my head. *She's been acting strangely for weeks.*

The birthday party. The stalking. Suddenly it all fits.

'I'm a copy of a copy,' I say.

'What?'

'Six weeks ago, Ares realized that Graeme had the QMP. But they couldn't figure out exactly where he was keeping it, because the basement muffled the signal from the tracking beacon. The house has incredible security, so they couldn't break in to look for it and, if they bribed him or threatened him, he might go to the police. Detective Anders was already sniffing around.'

'How do you know that?'

'At school, she showed me some videos of weapons, which I later saw in Ares' headquarters. Anyway, they must have been wary of kidnapping or torturing Graeme at that stage. They wouldn't want anyone else to know they'd lost it and a missing senior defence staffer would have raised suspicions. So instead they built a listening device. A walking, talking replica of his daughter. Then they intercepted the real Chloe on her way home from Pete's birthday party, killed her and made the switch.'

'That's insane,' Becky says.

'Think about it. Graeme trusted Chloe. The replica—Chloe Two—could go into every room of his house, use his car and listen to all his conversations without making him suspicious. She was bound to overhear something useful.'

'You think Chloe Two was spying on him for Ares?'

'Not intentionally,' I say. 'I think they just gave her really good ears and programmed her to be curious. The craziest part is that their plan nearly worked. If Chloe Two had survived, she might have overheard Graeme talking to Nadine, just like I did. When Ares picked her up and scanned her hard drive, they'd know everything that I know now.'

'You don't know where the QMP is, though' Becky points out.

'Only because it's not in Graeme's basement any more. That's the part I can't figure out.'

'Why would Ares have to collect Chloe Two to find out what she knew? Couldn't they have designed her to transmit what she saw and heard wirelessly?'

'The house is a fortress,' I remind her. 'For all Ares knew, a rogue transmission would have set off an alarm. Instead, they must have dispatched a small group of soldiers to observe Chloe Two from a distance and pick her up when the time was right. They messed that up the night she died and they haven't got to me either. Yet.'

'You don't think she knew she was a machine?'

'No. Nor did I, when I first woke up. They probably used the same template for her software that she used for mine.'

'Wouldn't she have figured it out, though?' Becky asks.

My lungs tighten in my chest, even though I know they're not there.

'No,' I say. 'Why would she? I can eat. I can spit. I can sense my heartbeat. I feel real—and I was made out of bits and pieces ordered over the internet. She was manufactured by a billion dollar company which specializes in robotics. Her body would have been much more realistic than mine.'

'But because she was curious, she noticed the soldiers following her. And instead of telling anyone . . .'

'She built me. Chloe Three. Now that I think about it, that's exactly the sort of solution a machine would come up with.'

'That's why you had no memory of me,' Becky realizes. 'Because the Chloe who created you wasn't the same one I had a relationship with.'

'Exactly. Even if Ares hacked into Chloe's email, and her phone, and her social profiles, they wouldn't have known about you—so Chloe Two didn't know either.'

Becky is silent for a moment. I wonder if she's thinking about Chloe One. The girl she loved. The girl who died only hours after their first kiss. The girl who was more than I could ever be.

'So what do we do?' she asks finally.

'I've got an access card. I'm on my way to Hera Global.'

'*What?* No! We have to go to the police.'

'We don't have a shred of proof,' I say. 'But if I can get into their server room . . .'

'You *are* the proof.'

'Ares didn't build me,' I say. 'Chloe Two did. Even if Anders believes me after she finds out what I am, Ares has an army of lawyers to protect them. I need their email records.'

'At least take some time to plan. You can just . . .'

'I have a plan, and it can't wait. Soon they'll start to wonder what happened to the soldier who kidnapped me. They'll revoke his access card.'

'Chloe, listen to me. They have hundreds of soldiers. They'll kill you.'

The desperation in her voice makes me realize that she actually cares. To her, I'm more than just her girlfriend's ghost.

But Ares murdered Graeme, Nadine, and two Chloes. They tortured me. They nearly killed Pete. And now that they know who I am, they could come after Kylie or Henrietta. This is my last chance to stop them from hurting anyone else.

'You forget,' I say, trying not to sound sad. 'I'm not alive.'

'Chloe . . .'

'I can get in and try to hack their servers, but I need a way out afterwards,' I say. 'Can I borrow your brother's skateboard?'

~

Ten minutes later, I'm parking the van a few houses up from Chloe's place and hoping her immediate neighbours won't notice it. I jog to her front door and slip inside.

'Mum?'

No answer. She's out.

I run into Chloe's room, grab her backpack, and drop Thomas's gun inside. Slinging the bag onto my shoulder, I hurry back out into the kitchen, where I tear a sheet of paper from a pad, pluck a pen from a dusty coffee mug, and write *Gone for walk, back soon. Chloe.*

That should buy me enough time to do what I need to do.

I dash to the front door and pull it open.

Kylie is standing there with her keys in her hand and a shopping bag in the other. Dark rings circle her eyes. She's been crying again.

A sharp ache forms in my chest.

202

'Mum,' I say.

'Hi,' she says. 'Is everything OK?'

'Sure. I'm just going for a walk.'

Kylie looks sceptically at the fading sky. 'It'll be dark soon,' she says.

'I know. I won't be long.'

'What's in the bag?'

I try to keep the panic out of my voice. 'We got some mail for a neighbour. A parcel. I thought I'd drop it off on the way.'

'Are you sure everything's OK?'

'Yes,' I say, hating myself for the lie. 'I'll be back soon, OK?'

'OK.'

I pretend not to notice her staring as I jog away. It's not until she's out of sight that I start thinking about what I'm about to do.

I wish I'd said goodbye properly. I wish I'd written *Love you* on the note. I probably won't make it home.

~

The last rays from the setting sun glance off the sloped wall of the glass tower, turning my windscreen an ominous orange as the van trundles up the street. The roller door—or where it used to be, before I cut it up with a helicopter—is about sixty seconds away. Sixty chances to turn back. Once I'm inside, I can't back out.

Fifty-nine chances. Fifty-eight.

I don't take any of them. Ares is a menace, and I'm the only one in a position to do something about it.

The roller door has been replaced by a temporary boom gate, which the van could probably break through. But I want to stay unnoticed as long as possible, so I ease the van to a halt in front of the gate, and push the button on the intercom.

'Powdered wood,' the intercom says.

'Stitches new,' I reply in the soldier's voice, hoping that they haven't changed passwords.

'Mission status?'

'Successful.'

'Passengers?'

I hesitate. Once he had the QMP, was the soldier ordered to kill me, or to bring me in for interrogation?

'None,' I say.

There's a pause.

The boom gate starts to rise, and fear clenches in my abdomen as I realize how close I came to being executed.

I'm about to enter the office of a company which will try to murder me as soon as they realize I don't have what they want. Every instinct screams to drive the van back up the alley. I don't know how many other people they have slaughtered.

But nor do I know how many more people will die if I don't stop them. I put the van into first gear and roll it down the ramp.

The car park is devoid of people, but full of vehicles. Sedans, vans, four-wheel drives, as well as the gun-mounted Jeep and assortment of bomb-disposal robots. I park the van in an empty space, climb through into the back, and roll up the carpet to reveal a spare tyre. It's surprisingly heavy—it takes three attempts to pull it out of the space and reveal what I really want, which is the L-shaped bar used for tightening the nuts on the outside of the wheel. I drop the tyre iron into Chloe's backpack alongside Becky's skateboard and jump out of the van, the soldier's Browning 9mm in my hand.

Taking aim at the tyres of the vehicles around me, I pull the trigger. The muzzle flashes and snaps like a hammer hitting a snare drum, twice, three times, over and over until it clicks empty and stops kicking in my hand.

The vehicles settle down on their deflated tyres. If I'm followed when I leave here, it will be on foot.

It's not until the deafening echoes and the hissing of punctured rubber fade away that I realize my throat has started clicking again like a broken pair of headphones. I clamp my mouth shut until the sound dissipates, wondering how much longer my mechanical body will last.

The clicking feels like a bad omen. The first time it happened, Ares soldiers showed up at Scullin High as though summoned.

I approach the door to the main building and try the handle. It's locked. I hold the soldier's access card out in front of the sensor and try again, but it doesn't work. I hear the sound of an alarm coming faintly from somewhere inside the building

~

I slam my fist against the door. The impact thrums through my titanium skeleton. I've only just arrived, and already the mission is a failure.

The lift. I could try going up that way.

I run over to it. The call button clicks uselessly. When I press my ear against the steel, there's only silence from beyond. Perhaps the lifts are always inactive at this time of night.

The air vent is too narrow to fit through and covered by a thin grille. But as I stare at the rusted pop rivets, an idea forms in my head.

I belt the grille with the tyre iron until it's loose enough to pry out of the frame, making enough room to push my backpack through into the darkness. Then I take off my clothes and tell myself that the pain I'm about to experience is an illusion.

My arm twists around and around and around and then pops off. I toss it through the hole and then get to work on my legs.

It feels like performing an autopsy on myself. Each thigh rotates one thousand and eighty agonising degrees before detaching from my hip joints. Lying on the floor, little more than a torso, I feed both legs into the hole.

With only one arm, my shoulders should be narrow enough—but my hips are still too wide. Lifting them into the air with my abdominal muscles, I use my remaining arm to twist them around until they're loose enough to be removed. I pick up my hips, turn them sideways so as they will fit, push them through the ventilation shaft and drag myself in after them, moving like a misshapen caterpillar.

For a horrifying moment, I think I'm not going to be able to squeeze through. I'll be stuck here as a triple amputee until Ares finds me. But my head and shoulders are just small enough to squeeze through the gap.

When my face emerges into the lift shaft, I see movement. Rats, perhaps. But no. It's my severed limbs, twitching like partially dissected frogs. Becky did say I had Wi-Fi—I must be controlling them remotely. Disturbing.

It takes a few minutes to reassemble myself in the lift shaft and put my clothes back on. I waste precious seconds accidentally attaching my left leg to my right hip and then cursing as I have to unscrew it again.

There are no lights, and no ladders. No way up, except by climbing the cables. But I have high-grip rubber hands, and a battery that hasn't failed me yet. The soldier said the servers were on the top floor, so that's where I'm headed.

I glance at Chloe's watch. Becky is parked by the sloped side of the building with her mum's trailer. I told her to leave if I'm not out by eight o'clock. It's six-forty now.

I clamber warily onto the iron counterweight, remembering what Fresner said about how magnets could damage computers. Then I start climbing.

~

After fifteen minutes I'm at the very top of the lift shaft. My hands and feet are burning. Before I started climbing, I kicked off my shoes and put them in my backpack so I could use my silicone arches. This made the ascent easier on my muscles but harder on my skin.

I cling to the steel cables, staring at a pair of sliding doors that are slightly out of reach. No pipes to grip, no platform to stand on while I force the doors open, and it's a long, long way down. The lift shaft is an open mouth below me, waiting to swallow my body and pulverize it when I hit the bottom.

I try a practice swing, but the cable is too taut to move very far. While my feet can almost reach the sliding doors, my fingertips have no hope.

The lift car itself is suspended in the gloom to my left, one floor below me. Perhaps I can swing onto the emergency access hatch on the roof. I slide about a metre down the cable to get some more slack, and then kick my legs to get momentum.

It's no use. My feet can't quite reach the car. I'm going to have to jump.

207

I wriggle out of my backpack and toss it across. It soars over the yawning cavern and lands on top of the car with a *thunk*.

The cables creak as I swing back and forth, a little further each time. Soon I'm swaying like a pendulum, a hundred metres above certain death. At the bottom of the fifth swing I fling myself loose.

For a heart-stopping moment I hang above the deadly pit, my legs pedalling in the empty air, and then I hit the top of the car.

My feet skitter across the metal. Too late, I realize I'm about to pitch over into the shaft on the other side. I take a swipe at the cables connecting the car to the pulleys above, and miss. My legs step into the void, and I feel myself plunging downwards.

Desperate, I throw out a hand, and catch the edge of the car just as I'm nearing the point of no return. My chest bashes against the side of it, and my shoulder joint nearly comes loose again, but I grab the car with my other hand and drag myself back up to safety.

The speaker in my throat is making heavy breathing sounds, which echo all around the shaft. I silence them. Holding my breath indefinitely no longer unnerves me.

I slide back the bolt and lift the emergency access hatch to reveal polished tiles, a thick safety bar, and mirrors on the walls to ease claustrophobia. No people, thankfully.

I drop into the car, feeling less safe than I usually do in a lift. Having seen the steel strands that suspend the car and the deadly void below it, it's hard not to imagine being trapped in here during a free fall.

When I touch the button for the top floor, it starts to rise immediately. Whatever stopped me from summoning the car to the ground level, apparently it doesn't affect commands made from inside. I can hear the whirring of the pulleys as the lift approaches the top, and the hissing of the brakes as it stops.

The doors slide open. I listen to the silence for a moment before poking my head out into the corridor. No one is here. Only my blurred reflection moves in the brushed-steel panelling of the walls.

My relief is tempered by unease. I'm creeping into the sleeping lion's den, waiting to hear a roar.

I bundle up Chloe's jacket and jam it between the lift doors to stop them closing. Then I go left up the corridor, looking for the server room.

A narrow door is set into the wall on my right with a keyhole but no handle. It looks like a cleaning supply cupboard, but I give it a push anyway. Locked. I could break into it with the tyre iron, but that would be noisy. If I don't find what I'm looking for anywhere else, I'll come back.

The corridor dead ends up ahead with an unmarked door, bigger than the last one. Ares Security probably wouldn't signpost their server room, so I have a good feeling about it.

I try the handle. Unlocked. The door swings open, and I step through.

But there are no servers in here.

Just a teenage girl in a cage with thick bars.

She stares at me. I stare at her.

It's only when she screams that I realize I'm looking at the real Chloe Zimetski.

IMPOSTOR

'What . . . ?' Chloe screeches. 'What are you?'

She's dressed in the same long woollen jumper and short skirt that she wore to Pete's birthday party. Her feet are clad in a pair of slippers, which she must have put on after she got home, but before Ares took her.

The only things in her cage are a plastic water bottle, a muesli bar wrapper, a toilet with no seat, and a thin camping mattress. The light bulb is above the top of the cage, casting zebra stripes of darkness across the floor.

She smells terrible. Ares has fed her, but I guess a shower was out of the question.

As the door swings closed behind me, Chloe shrinks back into the corner of the cage, still screaming.

I shush her. 'I'm here to help you.'

She doesn't look reassured. 'Please,' she begs, 'I've already told you everything I know. Whatever this is, don't do it.'

I've been stupid. I should have been asking myself how Ares got all Chloe One's memories into Chloe Two. If I had thought about it, I would have guessed that Ares had interrogated her before killing her. That might have led me to wonder why they would kill her at all.

I get it now. There was no girls' development camp. Ares made it up, to cover Chloe's absence for a couple of days while they interrogated her. No wonder Graeme and Kylie complained that she hadn't told them about it in advance.

I look around the rest of the room for a camera or a microphone, but I can't see one. A couch squats in the corner. A silent TV hangs behind thick glass on the opposite wall.

Avenging Graeme's death can't take precedence over saving his daughter's life. I have to get her out of here.

'Listen to me,' I say. 'I'm not one of them. Ares built a copy of you. I am a copy of that copy. I'm here to help you escape.'

'Please don't kill me,' she says.

What can I say to make her trust me? Anything at all could be a trick. She's told Ares every detail about her life.

Except one.

'Becky sent me,' I say.

Her eyes widen. 'What?'

'Becky helped me get in here. Now I'm going to get you out.'

Hopeful tears rain down Chloe's cheeks. 'Where is she?'

'She's waiting for you,' I say, stretching the truth a bit. 'Just tell me how to open the cage, and we'll go.'

'You, uh . . . ' She points to a green rubber button behind me. 'That unlocks it.'

I slam my palm down on the button. Something clanks inside the cage door, and Chloe pushes it. She's so weak that it barely moves, so I grab it and swing it open.

Chloe steps out shakily. I wonder how long she's been in there—probably since the night of the party. Six weeks. It's amazing that she's not crazy.

'Follow me,' I say, and I twist the handle of the door which leads to the corridor.

It won't turn.

'Oh no,' Chloe says. 'Oh no, oh no!'

I struggle with the door. 'Why won't it open?'

'It only opens from the outside,' she whispers.

There are no other doors. No windows. No tools.

We're stuck here.

~

I try to call Becky, but my phone has no reception. I had the same problem in the basement—Ares must have some kind of blocking system in place.

A small locker stands in the corner of the room. When I rattle the handle, Chloe says, 'Don't.'

'What's in there?' I ask.

She looks away.

It's locked, so I don't pursue the issue any further. She and I have been standing in silence for about three minutes when she says, 'They killed my Dad, didn't they?'

I hesitate, and then nod. 'I'm really sorry.'

She shuts her eyes. 'They dragged him in here so he could see me. They said they knew he was going to give something to the defence minister. Then they said they'd slit my throat in front of him if he didn't give it to them. He said he'd do anything, but he didn't have what they were looking for. They took him away after that.' She grabs my arm. 'Is Mum OK?'

'She misses Graeme,' I say. 'But she's safe.'

'When was the last time you talked to Dad?'

'Uh, the day before yesterday.'

'What did he say?'

'I told him I was going to hang out with Becky. He said, "I just want you to be safe."'

It's not until I see the shock in Chloe's eyes that I realize I said this in Graeme's voice.

'I'm sorry,' I say again.

'If they murdered him,' she says, 'then why have they kept me alive?'

Chloe's right. From the moment they killed Graeme, she was no longer useful as a bargaining chip. Ares must be keeping her alive for a secondary purpose.

My guess is that once they had the QMP, they planned to dispose of me and leave Chloe's body in my place. They would make her death look like an accident, just as they had done with Graeme.

'I don't know,' I lie.

'You were living with them,' she says. 'Mum and Dad, and Becky, and Henrietta.'

'Yes.'

'This whole time, I thought they'd be so worried about me. But they didn't even know I was missing.'

I shake my head.

'I guess that's good.' A tear trickles down her cheek. 'I don't want them to be sad.'

'They won't be,' I say. 'When we get out of here . . .'

'We're never getting out of here,' Chloe says. 'Don't kid yourself. We can't call for help. This door only opens from the outside. And when it does, the guards will . . .'

'Shhh.' Footsteps. Coming closer.

Chloe's right. I can't get us both out of here. But maybe I can save her.

I step into her cage, and slam the door. She's locked out, and I'm locked in.

She boggles at me. 'What are you doing?'

'Give me your jumper.'

'You can't . . .'

'Hide behind the couch. When the guard comes in, sneak out of the door behind him. There's a lift further down the corridor. Take it to the basement, climb under the boom gate, and then run as fast as you can until you find the police.'

The footsteps are almost at the door.

'I can't fool them unless I'm wearing your jumper,' I say. 'Hand it over.'

Chloe tears off the woollen garment, throws it to me, and ducks behind the couch.

I pull the jumper over my chest and throw myself onto the mattress just as the door opens. A soldier enters—one I recognize. His tattooed neck marks him as the soldier who shot Chloe Two.

'Get up,' he says. His voice is like corrugated iron.

'Why?' I ask.

'Just do it.'

The door starts to fall closed behind him. At the last second, I see Chloe's hand snake out from behind the couch and block it.

'Am I getting an upgrade?' I ask. 'Are you moving me to the presidential suite?'

Chloe rises to her feet behind him. A mistake. It sounds like he's about to unlock the cage, and when he turns around to push the button he'll see her.

'Or perhaps one of your men has gone missing,' I say, desperate to distract him. 'The guy with the bruises on his chin. You're moving me, because you think he might have defected.'

The soldier stares at me. 'What do you know about that?'

Chloe slips through the door behind him.

'I heard some of the guards talking about it,' I say.

He's not entirely convinced. He looks me up and down, and his eyes pause on my jeans. Chloe was wearing a skirt.

'Where did you get those?' he asks.

I try to look as though that's the dumbest thing I've ever heard. 'A shop in Garema Place. But I don't think they'd have them in your size.'

The soldier walks over to the locker. The one Chloe was afraid to look at. He pulls a key from his pocket.

'In a minute, I'm going to ask you that question again,' he says. 'And you're going to tell me the truth.'

He pulls out a car battery and a pair of jump leads. The teeth of the alligator clips glint at me.

'Where did you get those jeans?' he asks.

I edge away from the cage door. 'I bought them. I've been wearing them this whole time. Why do you care about them now?'

He attaches one of the jump leads to the battery. When he taps the alligator clip against the bars of the cage, a shower of sparks lights up the room. My skin begins to tingle.

'Who has been feeding you information?' he demands.

'I don't know his name,' I cry. 'He's just some guy I overheard talking!'

He steps back and pushes the button to unlock the cage.

I'm not going to stand back and wait for him to torture

me. So I run at him, crashing through the cage door and swiping for his eyes with my plastic fingernails.

He yells, but hopefully not loud enough for the other soldiers in the building to hear him. For a second I think I'm winning—then he grabs my throat and slams me against the wall.

'You've been in here for six weeks,' he hisses. 'How do you know what's going on outside?'

There's nothing I can say to get myself out of this.

'Screw you,' I reply.

He jams the alligator clip into my neck and there's a buzzing sound . . .

~

I can't move my legs. Or my hands. I can't even turn my head. Someone has glued me to the wall.

No, they haven't. I'm a severed head on a shelf.

The sight is horribly familiar. My headless body is slumped on the floor. My captor taps at the keys of a laptop. But this time it's not Chloe Zimetski, nor a machine that looks like her. It's Warren Christiansen, CEO of Ares Security and majority shareholder of Hera Global.

'I don't understand,' he mutters to himself. 'How did this happen?'

I'm in the same room as before, but the door has been propped open so as not to trap Christiansen inside. I can see the lifts. Escape is so close—but I'm immobilized. I don't feel like much time has passed. Ten minutes, perhaps. Not long enough. Even if Chloe got away, it's not enough time for her to have alerted the police.

The soldier with the tattoos stands behind Christiansen, looking at the screen. 'What's wrong?'

Christiansen's voice is thick and sonorous. 'My AI script was one of the founding technologies of this company. After we took out Chloe Zimetski, I told my developers to install the same software on the replica. But this isn't it.'

He thinks I'm Chloe Two. He doesn't realize she made a duplicate of her own.

'Maybe the developers wrote a new AI programme,' the soldier suggests.

'No,' Christiansen says. 'Someone must have got to her before you could bring her in. Her software has been interfered with.'

'Shall I take her to be recycled, then?'

'No. Not all her files are corrupted. The memories we inserted of the development camp are intact, for example. Graeme and Nadine turned out to be useless. The replica is our only hope of extracting the QMP's location.'

He turns back to the computer and keeps typing.

Every keystroke brings me closer to an electronic lobotomy. But maybe I can stall him, giving time for the real Chloe to come back with reinforcements.

'Stop messing with my brain,' I say, 'and I'll tell you everything you want to know.'

Both men glance over sharply.

'You're awake,' Christiansen says.

I try to nod, but it doesn't work without a neck. 'I'm willing to make a deal.'

A thin smile. 'You don't have much to bargain with.'

'Why are you taking to it like it's not a machine?' the soldier asks.

'"Her", not "it",' Christiansen says. 'She's every bit as complex as you or me.'

'I have information,' I say. 'I know why that software is unfamiliar to you. I know where the real Chloe Zimetski is, and I know where the QMP ended up.'

This last part isn't true, but it was the right thing to say. Hunger lights up his eyes.

'Where?' he asks.

'I'll tell you—once you've agreed to a few conditions.'

He gestures at the computer. 'I've been going through your hard drive. You don't know where it is.'

'As you can see, I've modified my programming. Even if you found the hidden files I created, it would take years to crack the encryption. Your only option is to negotiate.'

'Intriguing,' he says, smiling. 'Go on, then. What are your conditions?' he asks.

'I want your word,' I say, 'that you'll let me go, and the real Chloe Zimetski and her mother will be unharmed.'

He hesitates. He knows that if he agrees too readily, I'll realize that he's lying.

'You're in no position to make demands,' he says. His hand strays back to the keyboard. 'It wouldn't take much to wipe your brain.'

'I have nothing left to lose,' I say. 'But you do. Erase my memories and you'll never find your billion dollar investment.'

The soldier watches this exchange with growing unease.

'Very well,' Christiansen says. 'I accept your terms. Tell me where the QMP is.'

'Not so fast,' I say, still stalling. 'How do I know I can trust you?'

'I lose nothing letting you go free,' he replies. 'Why would I waste resources keeping you here?'

'You kept the real Chloe Zimetski here for six weeks, and she needed to eat,' I say.

His eyes narrow. 'You seem to be under the impression that I'm the bad guy here. But someone stole from me and I tried to put that right in the most painless way possible.'

No one is looking at my headless body. I flex, and watch a finger twitch.

'If you're not the bad guy,' I ask, 'why did Nadine steal the QMP?'

'Simple greed, I imagine. As you say, it's worth billions.'

'Why can't you just build another one?'

'You're missing the point,' Christiansen says. 'We can't let a QMP fall into anyone else's hands. They could hack into any bank, any government database—it would be a security nightmare. We're trying to protect this country.'

'The government has been paying you record-breaking amounts of money to protect this country lately. That wouldn't be because you hacked into their databases and copied all their classified data, would it?'

Christiansen opens his mouth. Hesitates.

'How does it work, exactly?' I ask. '"Hire my troops or I'll let WikiLeaks access my servers?"'

It looks like he's deciding whether or not to deny it. I keep pushing.

'You need the QMP because if anyone else gets it,' I say, 'they can prove that you committed treason. And if the government finds out that you don't have it any more, they'll know they can communicate without you listening in. They'll start working on a plan to take you out.'

'Enough.' Christiansen turns his hands over, palms up. 'What do you want?'

'I want a recording of this conversation,' I say. 'I can't show it to anyone because they'll realize I'm a machine. You can't show it to anybody because it proves you blackmailed the defence force. That way, we're both safe.'

Christiansen strokes his chin. He's about to say something when the soldier's radio crackles.

'Sir! The federal police are here.'

The soldier's eyes widen. He presses his radio to his face. 'Say again.'

'I have fifteen federal police officers in the lobby, led by a Detective Anders. They have a warrant.'

Chloe. She did it.

The soldier's face is ashen. He's about to say something when Christiansen snatches the radio out of his hands.

'Let them up,' he says, smiling. 'And remind Anders that the last time she came in here with her unprovable accusations, it cost the government six hundred thousand dollars in damages.'

He put the radio down. 'This changes nothing,' he says.

He and the soldier are both looking at my head. This is my chance.

Behind them, my headless body climbs to its feet. It picks up the car battery and the jump leads.

'This changes everything,' I say, to keep their attention on my face. 'You think the cops are going to ignore what you're doing to me? You don't think they'll see the cage?'

My body slips out of the open door behind them. I try to turn it towards the lifts, but it spins the wrong way. This is like trying to write by hand while watching myself in the mirror.

'You're a machine,' Christiansen says. 'I can do what I like with you. And, as you just worked out, no branch of the government can touch us, because we have copies of all their secret data. Plus, we own a law firm, a media conglomerate, and the best politicians that money can buy. The police can't come after us and they know it.'

When my headless body is facing the right way, I put down the car battery, press my palms against the lift doors and pry them far enough apart to get my foot into the gap. From this angle, I can just make out the blackness of the empty lift shaft.

I pick up the jump leads again.

'You shouldn't have killed Graeme Zimetski,' I say.

'He shouldn't have stolen the QMP from me,' Christiansen replies.

What I'm about to do will kill me. But it will stop Ares from hurting anyone ever again.

I meet Christiansen's eucalyptus eyes. 'You clearly don't understand ethics,' I say, 'but you understand consequences. So let me put it another way.'

My voice gets louder. 'You should have bought off-site backup servers.'

I tap the jump leads against the cables in the lift shaft. A blast of electricity zaps down to the iron counterweight.

And all the lights go out.

THE HEADLESS HORSEWOMAN

I'm not dead.

The electrified iron block should have created enough magnetism to wipe every computer in the building—erasing all Ares' stolen data—but somehow I'm still functioning.

I can feel it, though. The magnet has its own gravity. It feels like the centre of the Earth.

The soldier is yelling into his radio. 'We're under attack! Shoot to kill!'

Christiansen is glaring at me. 'What did you do?' he roars.

I open my mouth, and scream.

Both men cover their ears and squeeze their eyes shut, as though the ultrasonic shriek is blinding as well as deafening. I keep screaming as my headless body stumbles back into the room.

I snatch up my backpack with one hand and my head with the other. The world is a shadowy, lopsided maze. As I try to flee, the soldier grabs me and pushes me against the wall.

I try to clobber him with my bag, but I've got my left and right arms mixed up. I end up bashing him over the head with my own skull. Fireworks of pain explode out of my forehead, but the soldier gets it worse, since he doesn't have titanium beneath his skin.

He collapses, and I stagger out of the room.

To find twenty soldiers pointing guns at me.

This looks like it might be all of Ares' local troops. I'm surrounded by dozens of cruel mouths and goggled eyes. Everyone is armed—some with handguns, others with assault rifles or shotguns, many with flash grenades hanging from their belts.

'Get down on the ground,' one of them yells. 'Face down.'

Maybe I can get back out the door before they shoot me. But they would just chase me, and some of them are bound to be faster.

A shot booms through the corridor. I cry out as a round clips my arm, carving out a chunk of silicone muscle. It's like being hit by a droplet of molten lava.

I drop my bag and raise my hands. As my head rises in my grip, it feels like I've grown taller by half a metre. I fall to my knees, wobbling as though drugged. Then I pitch forwards, crashing into one of the soldiers and landing face down on the floor.

It takes the soldier a moment to realize I swiped the pins out of her flash grenades on the way down. I scuttle back and throw myself behind a partition in the wall behind me.

'Hey, wait . . . ' she says.

And then the corridor goes white.

Even through closed eyelids, the simultaneous denotation of the three flash grenades is like looking directly into the sun. The blast of sound is deafening for a fraction of a second, then it's replaced by pure silence. The microphones in my ears must have overloaded.

I scramble to my feet, grab the bag and my head and sprint away from the soldiers. My feet slap the tiles as I race past the lift, hoping to find a stairwell. A door awaits me at the other end of the corridor. I hit it at a run, shoving it open, and find myself standing in a jungle of computer towers linked by a vineyard of data cables. This must be the server room. I'm relieved to see that the computers are dark and silent, ruined by the magnetic pulse.

I shut the door behind me and run over to the window, willing Becky to still be in position. Please, please, please . . .

I look down. The glass is sloped, so it's hard to see, but Becky's mother's trailer is parked far, far below.

Something scuffles outside the door. The first of the soldiers scrambling to his feet.

I pull the skateboard out of Chloe's backpack and hold it in my trembling palm as I look for something to break the glass with. I can't believe I'm about to do this.

I hear the door flip open.

Gunfire erupts behind me. The window shatters as a stray round hits the glass. I hope Becky is under cover down below.

I'm not bulletproof. Chloe Two died after a shot to the skull. I hug my severed head to my chest, shielding it with my body.

Part of my belly explodes outwards, and I realize that I've been shot. Fragments of hot silicone splash out into the daylight.

The pain rushes up my chest like I'm being drawn and quartered. Another round punches through my shoulder.

My fear of bullets finally overwhelms my fear of heights.

And I leap through the remaining shards of glass.

I'm hanging in the air a hundred metres above the street . . .

~

Falling.

With the gravity from the electromagnet somewhere behind me, it feels like being upside down on the third loop of a roller coaster. I'm hurtling towards a fatal collision with the concrete far below, and I don't have much time to prepare.

Chloe's skateboard has slipped out of my hands. I reach through the spinning shards of glass, grab the board and push it against my feet. Soon I'm skating down the sloped side of the building at a terrifying pace, wheels clattering against window after window as I lean from side to side to try and make sure I land on target.

Far below me, Becky peers out the window of her mum's car, her jaw slack with amazement. She knew my escape plan, but hadn't expected me to be headless.

No time to meet her gaze. I'm not aiming for her, or the car, or the trailer.

I'm aiming for her brother's skate ramp.

The ramp is propped up against the side of the building, a little to my right. I lean sideways, trying to bend my trajectory towards it.

My head tumbles out of my grasp. As it spins, I can see the mottled sky, the surrounding buildings with the lights blown out by the magnet, the tiny cars trundling past beneath me and my headless body, skating down the polished windows and clutching at my head with one desperate hand.

I grab at my hair and pull my head under my arm.

Three. The board shudders beneath my feet.

Two. The blasting air is like a pillow over my face.

One. The ground rushes up to meet me.

I hit the ramp with such force that the glass behind it cracks and the wheels score two long grooves into the wood. All the momentum that should have flattened me against the footpath is deflected outward and, suddenly, I'm zooming across the street as if propelled by a rocket.

The asphalt growls under the wheels as I lean over, trying to swerve around a car even as it tries to swerve around me. The turn leaves me travelling parallel to it, but much, much faster. By the time the astonished driver slams her palm on the horn, I'm almost too far away to hear it.

Looking back, I see that Becky is already dragging the skate ramp back onto the trailer, like I told her to. She'll be gone by the time the soldiers or the police make it around to this side of the building. And with their tyres shot, Ares won't be able to give chase.

People stare in shock and bafflement as I skate past with my head under my arm. Someone yells, 'Oh my God!' Someone else laughs. As I vanish around the corner, I hear someone say, 'What was that advertising?'

I'm almost a whole block away before I come across some lights that are still on. It might be a while before Christiansen figures out exactly what I've done but, once he does, he'll realize it's irreparable. With no backup servers, all the stolen data is lost. Ares can no longer blackmail the government into hiring them. Nor can they protect themselves from prosecution. When the police find the cage on the top floor that will be the final nail in Ares' coffin.

An insane grin imprints itself on my face. I did it. I survived, I saved Chloe, and I protected my country from one of the biggest and most corrupt corporations in the world. Not bad for a collection of spare parts assembled in a teen girl's basement.

I just wish Graeme were alive to see Ares fall.

The skateboard has slowed down enough for me to step off. I jog alongside it for a few metres, shedding the extra momentum, and then stomp on the tail so it flips up into my hand. I'm already close to a kilometre away from the Hera Global head office. They'll never catch me now.

Putting my head back on is surprisingly fiddly, like trying to reseal a water bottle with cooking tongs. Once I've threaded the screw, I get dizzy watching the world spin.

Kylie must be worried. I told her I was going for a walk, and then disappeared for hours. Time to go back to the house and check on her.

I take the empty gun out of my bag, wipe off my fingerprints and throw it into a public bin. Then I jump back on the board and swerve onto the cycle path which Graeme used to take home.

EPILOGUE

'Hello?'

The house smothers me with its emptiness. Maybe Kylie got a call from the police. She might be picking Chloe up.

I haven't thought about what happens now. Kylie has her daughter back. Where does that leave me?

I step in and close the front door behind me. The bag and the board clunk to the floor. I walk into the bathroom, peel off my bullet-torn shirt and examine my torso in the mirror. The gunshot wounds go right through; I can see the wall behind me. But there's no pain. The artificial nerves must have died.

I'm lucky to be alive at all. The electromagnetic pulse from the electrified counterweight should have killed me, like it killed every other piece of electronics in the building.

They're not affected by electromagnetic pulses.

Do you know that for sure, or are you just guessing?

Guessing.

It's possible that a quantum computer might not be affected, but I'd have to look it up to be sure.

My jaw falls open. I keep staring at the mirror, but I'm no longer seeing it. Instead, I'm seeing all the things I should have noticed earlier.

The tracking device Thomas talked about. The clicking sound my throat made, shortly before Ares showed up at the school.

But most of the current designs are about the same size and shape as ordinary processors.

Graeme hid the QMP in the basement. Then Chloe Two built my brain out of bits and pieces she found down there. Later, Graeme couldn't find the QMP.

Is it possible that it's been inside my head all along?

I stare at my reflection, as though I'll be able to spot the world's most powerful computer behind my eyes. But all I see is glass.

~

In my bedroom, I take another top off the shelf and slip into it. The green cotton hugs my skin. I smooth it over the hole in my stomach, feeling absurdly self-conscious.

I wander back into the living room and sit on the couch, watching the street through the window. It feels like a long time since I've sat down.

I hear the tyres before I see the police car. It crawls into view and parks by the kerb without indicating.

Kylie gets out first. Her eyes are puffy and her nose is running. She says something to the cop behind the wheel, who nods gently and waves goodbye.

Becky and Chloe get out of the back seat.

They're holding hands.

They look so happy.

An ugly, wrenching feeling tears through my guts.

Before I know it, I'm running to the basement door, fumbling with the handle, stumbling down the stairs. I crouch down beneath the workbench, cowering in the darkness as though hiding from a bomb or a tornado.

Up above, the front door opens. I can hear voices.

'. . .just can't believe it,' Kylie is saying. 'Where is she?'

'She should be here,' Becky says. 'Chloe!'

Chloe says, 'You call her Chloe?'

'It's the only name she has.'

'Are you sure she made it out of the building?' Kylie asks.

'I saw her. The whole street saw her.'

'Maybe she's still on her way.'

'Maybe.'

Their feet clomp away into the living room.

I stare at the computer on which my brain was made, the nylon net which held me down, the vice which once held my severed head. When I was worried about how to escape. When I thought there was somewhere to escape to.

Someone walks back to the front door, alone. Stops.

The skateboard. I left it up there.

The basement door creaks open.

'Chloe?'

It's Becky's voice. I don't respond. The tears are cold on my cheeks.

She descends the steps, coming into view feet first. It only takes her a second to spot me.

She smiles. 'What are you doing?'

'Nothing,' I say. 'I just needed some space.'

'Not a lot of space under there,' she says. Then she sees the tears. 'Are you OK.'

'I'll be fine,' I say. My voice shakes. For the first time I can't control it. I no longer feel like a machine.

'I'm sorry,' Becky says. 'I had to tell them the truth.'

She thinks I'm still scared of being exposed as a machine. It hasn't even occurred to her that I'm hiding because I can't watch her love someone else.

Somehow, her ignorance hurts even more.

'I know,' I say. 'It's OK.'

'Detective Anders wants to talk to you. But she promised me you wouldn't be put in an evidence locker. She said you could stay with Chloe and Kylie. Legally, you'd be their property. You'd be safe.'

Property of Becky's girlfriend. Ageless plastic, watching the two of them grow old together.

'Can I tell Chloe and Kylie you're here?' Becky asks.

I shake my head miserably.

Becky sits on the concrete floor and puts her hand on my shoulder. 'You saved Chloe's life. They want to thank you.'

'There's no room for me here.'

'They can turn the study into a bedroom. I can help.'

'There's no room in their lives. Kylie has her daughter back. You have your girlfriend. Chloe has her freedom. None of you need me any more.'

Becky hugs me. Her hair clouds my face. 'There's room for you,' she says. 'I promise. OK?'

Chloe and I are not the same person. It's a cruel coincidence that we fell for the same girl.

Perhaps it was inevitable. Becky is smart, and kind, and braver than she realizes. She deserves a human girlfriend.

I kiss her. Just on the cheek, just briefly enough to let her think that it's nothing more than a thank you. Then I let her go.

'OK,' I say.

She beams, and stands up. I climb out from under the workbench.

She puts one foot on the stairs. 'Coming?'

'I'm right behind you.'

I follow her up the stairs. When she opens the basement door, she turns right and walks away towards the living area. I turn the other way, and slip out of the front door. I don't know if she hears me. Without looking back, I dart across the grass, sprint out onto the street and jog towards the mountain ranges, leaving the lights of the city far behind.

ACKNOWLEDGEMENTS

I owe a tremendous debt to arts ACT and the ACT government. Without their support, I would be working in a call centre and *Replica* would be a half-finished manuscript on a flash drive somewhere.

I also want to thank and congratulate the team at Oxford University Press, particularly Clare Whitston and Claire Westwood, who pushed this book over the finish line.

My amazing agent, Clare Forster at Curtis Brown Australia, believed in this book from the beginning. She, Annabel Blay, and Stephanie Thwaites at Curtis Brown London toiled long and hard to find the right publisher for it. All of you have my gratitude.

I'd like to acknowledge my kind friends Maria Bernardi, Lisa Berryman, Claire Craig, Belle Evans, Paul Kopetko, Chris MacPhillamy, and Dylan Slater who provided crucial feedback on early drafts.

Lastly, I want to thank my family—Barbara, Ian, Tom, and my wonderful wife, Venetia—who never gave up on me.

ABOUT THE AUTHOR

Jack Heath was born in 1986 in Sydney, Australia, and lived in Wollongong and Melbourne before settling in Canberra, where *Replica* is set.

He has been shortlisted for Young Australian of the Year, the Nottinghamshire Brilliant Book Award, and the National Year of Reading 'Our Story' collection, as well as Best Sci-fi Novel and Best YA Short Story at the Aurealis Awards.

Jack lives with his wife, their Staffordshire terrier, and several chickens.

He is not, as far as he is aware, a robot.